The Husband

Don DeBon

Dedicated to all that I drove crazy while writing this book.

Contents

—1—

Erin walked to the window and gazed out towards the woods as it began to rain. It had been three hours since they fought, and he still had not returned. But as she was reaching for the phone, a dark shadow flashed past the edge of her vision. She turned but saw nothing but the line of trees.

The back door rattled.

Erin ran downstairs and grabbed the baseball bat in the corner. The door handle rattled again as though someone had found their hidden key and was inserting it in the lock. She raised her bat.

The door opened with a crash revealing Jack's smiling face. "Love why did you lock the door?"

Erin let out a breath she didn't know she was holding while lowering the weapon. "Jack! You scared me to death. Why didn't you say something?"

"Sorry I thought you might be asleep. And by the looks of you, I think you were." He said pointing to the green teddy peeking out from beneath her robe.

She closed the robe quickly. "No, I was just upstairs reading. And will you get in here? You look soaked to the skin."

He smiled looking down at his check shirt and blue jeans. "I am. Got caught in the rain when I was walking back." He stepped inside and closed the door.

The cold air made Erin's skin pebble as a chill ran through her. She shivered. "Aren't you cold?"

"Of course. It is nasty out there." He said heading towards the steps.

"Let's get you in some dry clothes." Erin said padding his back causing tiny water droplets to fly off. "Wow you are soaked."

Jack turned smiling. "I told you."

A moment later they were in their bedroom. Jack walked over to the large dresser along the wall and pulled out the bottom drawer removing a clean pair of pajamas, then walked over to the bathroom.

Erin sat on the bed. "Jack? Where are you going? You can take them off here, we're married you know."

Jack laughed. "Of course, but I really need a hot shower." He said closing the door.

Erin heard water running and sighed. He was still mad at her, had to be. She couldn't take feeling this way. In their three years of marriage they had never fought like that. They always talked their way though it, he never left because he was so mad he couldn't stand the sight of her. She lay on the bed and hoped they could get past this. He was a good man, and she couldn't bear the thought of losing him.

The water stopped and a minute later the hair dryer started. Erin took another deep breath as the hair dryer stopped and Jack emerged from the bathroom wearing his blue pajama bottoms showing his chiseled form to perfection. "Jack, we have to talk."

"What about?" He said sitting down beside her.

"You know very well what about! I am sorry and I–"

He placed his hand on her exposed knee. "Love, I know. I was trying to make a joke and I see it was not the time. I only hope you can forgive me."

"Forgive you?! What is there to forgive, I realize it was all my fault."

Jack smiled. "It wasn't even though I know you feel that way. That teddy you haven't worn in months, and you know I love you in it. The instant I came in the door, I knew."

She sat up on the bed. "Jack, I–"

Jack put a finger on her lips. "Shhh my love, I know. And the fault is mine I should not have stormed out like that. I love you, nothing can ever change that. And let's not fight like that ever again."

Erin smiled sheepishly. "You sure you are not mad at me?"

He pulled the silk belt on her robe. It slid out with a satisfying fssssst allowing the robe to fall away and revealing lingeried form. He leaned forward and kissed her deeply then nibbled his way to her ear. "I am sure my love." He said pressing his body against hers until she went backwards onto the soft bed.

He smiled reached down and caressed the most tender spot beneath the thin fabric, moving back and forth back and forth.

"Ohhhh Jack," she moaned throwing her arms around his neck, then pressing her lips to his. She sucked on his bottom lip and managed to drink him in, his tongue caressing hers.

Jack reached up and slipped one of the straps down Erin's arm revealing her left breast. He cupped the feminine mound and using his thumb tenderly caressing the very tip. She shuddered under his touch as they grew in size.

He reached up and pulled the other strap off. His lips left her mouth and tenderly kissed his way down her neck, continuing onto her chest, then paused over her right breast. He smiled and kissed the tip. Then flicked it with his tongue over and over again.

Erin moaned as her eyes rolled back. He knew exactly where to touch.

Using both hands he slid the teddy past the swell of her hips revealing the treasure that was between her legs. Jack pressed himself up on his hands and knees over her naked form and kissed his way back up to her ear and breathed. "I love you my darling." He used a deep guttural tone that sent shivers through her body. Her heart hammered, and blood thundered in her veins.

Erin yanked Jack's pajamas down revealing the six pack he worked so hard at and his swelled, ready, manhood. She tried to pull him down with her arms but only managed to pull herself up. He smiled and leaned down nibbling her neck, working his way back up over her chin to her welcoming lips and proceeded to seed them with passion.

Erin burned with desire and she tried again to pull him down. She wanted him, no needed him inside. She needed to be one with the man, her husband, her love, the one that meant more to her than anything else in the world.

Another smile crossed Jack's lips, but he didn't stop loving her lips as he closed the distance between their hips. But then he paused a second, then another, and Erin wondered if this was all an act and he was still mad at her. That he was using this for his revenge. She would burn with desire for days if he stopped now. And he knew it.

But instead of pulling back, the very tip of him pressed against her entrance, then caressed it, tracing the line back and forth as he moved his hips. Erin's eyes rolled back again as several drops of moisture slipped out coating the tip of his manhood.

He continued the motion for several minutes causing Erin to wiggle in anticipation. When he felt she couldn't take anymore he slid inside. Erin gasped and kissed him harder. But then he stopped after his manhood only peeked inside her entrance. He pulled back out, traced the line and slid in a bit more. He repeated this several times until their bodies were fully one.

"Ohhhhhhhh Jackkkkk!" Erin moaned as he began to slide in and out faster and faster. Muscles were tightening, and she knew the edge was near. Heck, in the last few minutes she had never danced on the edge for so long.

Jack pulled her lips back with his and kissed her even more passionately than before. Her eyes rolled back again, and he pulled out as she shuddered and screamed digging her nails into his back. Without pause he slid back inside and continued even faster than before. "No! Not again! Please!" she shrieked.

He smiled and continued the fast pace. Erin's whole body shook as her eyes rolled back again, stars flashed behind them, and her internal muscles gripped him in another attack of pleasure. He exploded deep inside and her nails dug further into his back as her eyelids fluttered.

Erin's arms dropped and her eyes drooped as she lay utterly exhausted. Jack kissed her lips again. "You were wonderful my darling."

Her eyes shot open. "Me? You on the other hand, haven't made me feel like that in soooo long."

With a swift motion he flipped to her side and spooned her into his strong arms. "Yes you, my darling, were wonderful. And I love you so much." He paused pulling her closer, settling in along the curve of her back, and nibbled her ear. "I know I haven't told you that near enough."

Erin fought to keep her eyes open and managed to smile. "Yes you have, but I never grow tired of hearing it."

"And I hope you never will." He said reaching over with his left arm and flipped off the light.

"Trust me, I never will." She said as she turned her head, kissed his lips, snuggled into his arms, and closed her eyes. "What woman would?" she thought as sleep overtook her.

The glow was still apparent on Erin's face when she rolled over to find Jack missing. She pushed herself vertical and saw his pants from the previous night sticking out of the hamper. Sighing she reached over and grabbed her panties from the floor and tossed them into the hamper as well, then peeked out between the blinds. Jack's truck was still in the driveway. She picked up her phone and dialed. A second later she heard the unmistakeable dun da dun dun DUNNNN ringtone from his phone down in the study.

"Great, he didn't take his phone." She sighed again and walked into the bathroom.

Jane stopped. The woman in the mirror had a smile a mile wide. "I had better get rid of this grin before I see anyone today," she muttered. She hopped into the shower and turned on the massager on full force. Her body ached in places she didn't even know she had. But her grin widened when she thought about the cause, then it quickly disappeared. Jack had been good in bed yes, but never like that. She had tried to get him to understand what she wanted, without actually telling him. But even after years of marriage he hadn't got the message, and now he knew beyond what she could have dreamed? She blinked. Was it a dream?

She stepped out of the shower, toweled off, and wrapped it around her torso. Walking into the bedroom she checked the hamper. Jack's still-wet pants, shirt, socks, and boxers were all there. It wasn't a dream. But after last night, why would he leave her like some cheap one night stand?

She went to her dresser pulling out clean panties, a sports bra, pink t-shirt, and jeans. Perhaps a run would clear her mind.

Jogging down the dirt road a car pulled up alongside. "Hey girl, where are you headed?"

Erin looked over to her best friend Jane Seeliger. "Just out for a run," she said between breaths.

Jane's eyebrows met. "Something on your mind?"

"What do you mean? Can't a girl just go out for a run?"

Jane laughed. "You? Not unless you are trying to figure something out."

Erin stopped and bent over trying to catch her breath. "Dang it. You know me too well."

"Hop in girlfriend, free coffee and doughnuts on me."

"Doughnuts? How can I keep my figure eating those?"

"One won't hurt. And judging by the soaked shirt, you must have ran off three of 'em by now."

Erin's eyes drifted down, saw the drenched shirt, she nodded then threw her hair back while attempting to style it with her fingers. She leaned over still breathing hard. "All right, you win." She walked around to the passenger side of the little blue Volkswagen and got in.

A few minutes later they were sitting at the old scratched table in Jane's kitchen. She poured a hot cup of coffee from the pot and put a plate in front of Erin. Erin's eyes narrowed at the glistening doughnut.

Jane rolled her eyes. "We already talked about this. Will

you just eat it? I am sure you need something by the look of you."

"Don't you have something a little less …well …fattening?"

Jane rolled her eyes again. "Erin, you are not going to gain ten pounds by eating one doughnut. Something else is bothering you. I know you are careful with your diet, but not this bad."

Erin shifted in her seat. "It's nothing."

"Bull! I have known you long enough to tell when you fib. What is it? Did Jack hit you or something?"

"Oh no! Not at all!"

"Well then what is it?"

"Well …"

Jane sat down in the chair opposite Erin, placed her elbows on the table, and stuck her head between her arms. "Yessss?"

"It is just …"

"Erin for crying out–"

Erin's face turned bright red. "We made love last night," she muttered.

Jane threw her head back and laughed. "Are you kidding me? That is what has you all bent out of shape? Heck my husband hasn't paid attention to me in over a year. I sometimes wonder if he is gay!"

"It isn't that we did it, it is well …"

"Well what?"

"He did what I always wanted. I mean, more than I could have wanted. It was like a dream."

Jane smiled. "I can tell by the grin you now have. But so what? Isn't that was husbands are supposed to do? Love their wives?"

"Yes, you see it was like he saw my dreams and what I wanted. Or even more. Don't get me wrong Jack was always good, but not like this."

"Erin look, you had a wonderful night with your husband. Embrace that and don't worry about the rest. Heck, you have had more than I probably ever will. I sometimes wonder why I married the lump."

Erin smiled. "Because you love the lump."

Jane chuckled. "Yes, but don't tell him that. I would never hear the end of it."

"Tell you what, you don't tell Jack about this and I won't tell Blane," Erin said sipping the last of her coffee.

"Deal. Although, you know I would never tell this to anyone, regardless."

Erin smiled. "I know." She reached across the table and gripped Jane's hand. "Thank you girlfriend."

Jane gave a dismissive wave with her other hand. "What are best friends for?" Jane got up to put the dishes in the sink, then turned around. "Say, where is your stud-muffin of a husband, anyway?"

Erin blushed. "I don't know. I found him gone this morning."

Jane blew out a breath. "Just like a man to love and leave."

Erin shrugged. "He doesn't normally."

Jane crossed her arms over her chest and glared at Erin. "You mean to tell me that stud-muffin makes love to you on a regular basis and after an incredible night you are sitting here complaining? Gosh, I wish I had it so good!"

Erin's eyes fell down towards her toes. "When you say it like that, I am being rather silly aren't I?"

"Yeah, you are."

"It is strange though, he just left. I wonder where he went."

"By the sounds of it, doing something to surprise you would be my guess. Or he had to go to work."

Erin shook her head. "He doesn't work today. He is off for the next couple of weeks. Something to do with refurbishing the sawmill. His partner is taking care of the details so he could take a couple of weeks off."

"To be with you, I am guessing. I still stick by my original thought of him doing something to surprise you. I bet he will be there by the time you get home."

"You are probably right."

"Want a lift?"

Erin shook her head as she stood up. "Nah, I need to run off that doughnut."

Jane shrugged. "Suit yourself. But I still think you burned off three of them before I picked you up."

Erin walked over and gave her friend a hug. "I know, but I got to keep my figure for that stud-muffin," she said with a wink.

Erin left letting the screen door's spring snap it shut. She took off heading for home. The humidity had gone up in the last hour, but not awful. She peered towards the sky and saw angry clouds in the distance. The sky grew darker with each footfall and she managed to get home before the clouds dumped their drenching cargo.

The storm continued for hours while Erin busied herself around the house. Several bright flashes lit up the sky and thunder rattled the windows. "Jack, where are you?" she muttered. She decided to spend the time cooking him a special dinner. She spent hours on the steaks, different salads, and even managed to bake his favorite peanut butter cookies for dessert. She fully expected him home by five. Jack was never later than that, unless it was an emergency, and even then he always called. Erin set the table with lit candles and went upstairs to put on one of the short dresses she knew he liked. She came back down the stairs making clicking sounds as her heels played touch-and-go with the wood floor.

Erin sat down at the table, crossed her legs, and waited. But as time wore on she got angry. Two hours later she sighed, blew out what was left of the candles, dumped the food onto plates to microwave later, and went back upstairs to change.

Erin was washing the dishes when the old grandfather clock struck 8pm. Her eyes widened in near panic. She picked up her phone but spun around when the back door rattled.

With sun set being hours ago, there was only the dimmest of light showing when Jack came through the kitchen door.

"Jack!" Erin stood there in her jeans and t-shirt, set down the phone, crossed her arms, and on cue her foot started tapping. "Where were you?"

"Hmm? Oh in town helping Frank."

Erin stared. "Frank? How did you get there? The truck is still in the driveway."

"He called and offered to give me a lift."

"I was worried about you! Why didn't you call?"

Jack stepped forward and put his hands on her shoulders. "I am sorry love." She gazed back with an ice-cold glare. He started to sway her shoulders back and forth. "I really am sorry I didn't call. Frank had a real mess with a busted water line. Time got away from me."

Erin turned her head, eyes focusing on the black sky beyond the window. "You could have called. I made your favorite." Her eyes slid down to the floor.

Jack's eyes widened. "Rib-eye steaks? Really? I am sorry love. Really, I am." Jack sighed as he put his finger under her chin and guided her head back, then looked into her eyes. "Is there any way I can make it up to you?"

She tried to look away again, but he pulled her back. "Dang it! I need to be mad at him, but I never could resist that sad puppy dog look he does," she thought. Her eyes twinkled as she thought of the previous night. "Maybe," she said. Before Jack could ask, she leapt into his arms and kissed him so hard she thought she could feel his tonsils.

— 3 —

Erin smiled as she rolled over and found Jack smiling back. "Hello Mrs. Winecker. Did you sleep well?"

Her smile grew. "I did." She traced the lines on his face with her finger. "Did you?"

"I did. Tell you what, I will make breakfast. You rest and I will call when it is done."

Erin's eyebrows rose. "Breakfast? You?"

"Don't look so surprised. You know I can cook."

"Can yes, do ... no."

"Well I need to make up for yesterday."

Erin sat up still grinning. "Oh I think you did that last night."

"Good. But I still want to make you breakfast." Jack climbed out of bed and pulled on his pants. Erin's smile only grew at the short view of her nude husband. Her thoughts flashed back to the night before and how she loved to run her tongue up his six pack. Especially coated in chocolate, like it was last night.

"Okay, I will let you." She sat up in bed, but kept the sheet covering her breasts.

Jack smiled and pointed. "What? No free peek before I go slave over a hot stove?"

14

"Didn't you get enough last night?"

Jack walked over, bent down and kissed her lips. "Never my love." The kiss sent a shock wave through her and she dropped the sheet without thinking. "Now that is better," he said smiling. He leaned down further and kissed each breast then back up to her lips for another passionate kiss. "I will call when breakfast is ready. Eggs and bacon?"

Erin fought to come back to herself. "Yes that is–" But he was gone. She pulled herself out of bed. Every muscle ached, but in a good way. The thought that she definitely burned off any doughnuts after last night made her smile. Heck, she probably burned off a week's worth of doughnuts.

Erin made her way to the bathroom and after a long shower with the massager again on full, most of the aches were gone. She grabbed a clean pair of underwear, t-shirt, jeans, slipped them on, and walked down the stairs.

She found Jack in the kitchen wearing a pink lacy apron that said "Kiss the Cook." Erin always wondered what he would look like in it ever since he gave it to her one Christmas. But now seeing this beefy guy wearing such a feminine apron made her eyes hurt.

Jack continued scrambling the eggs but turned his head when Erin pulled a chair out from the table and sat down. He grinned and pointed to the stove. "I told you I would call. I got this you know."

"I know you do. But then I would have missed the fashion show."

Jack chuckled. "Well, how do I look?"

Erin winced. "Like one of those terrible Sci-Fi channel movies."

"That bad, eh?"

Erin shook her head. "No, worse."

"And here I thought I would surprise you."

Erin smiled. "You did, and I love you for it. I just can't say it was a good one."

Jack scooped up the eggs, put them on two plates, and slid on the bacon. "Here you are." He placed both plates on the table, took off the apron, hung it on the hook, then sat down. "There. I don't want to look like a Sci-Fi reject."

Erin giggled. "It was still worth it. I only wish I had my camera."

"Ha-ha, very funny. Now you are into blackmail?"

Erin laughed harder. "Well I am sure Ethan and the guys at work would love it."

Jack's eyes narrowed. "Not funny Erin."

"Yes it is," she said still giggling.

"Oh hush and eat your eggs. I hope you don't mind scrambled. You didn't say how you wanted them."

Erin's eyebrow rose. No she didn't, but she sure thought it. "This is fine. You know I like them scrambled."

"Yes I do. Say do you want to go on a picnic today?"

Erin tried not to choke on the eggs in her mouth. "Picnic? Today? I thought you were going fishing?"

"Yeah, I was. But then I thought how I have been spending so much time at work lately and neglecting my wife. Besides, I can go fishing with the guys anytime."

Erin's heart leapt into her throat. She had wanted to go on a picnic again with Jack for a long time. They hadn't been on one since they were dating. "Are you sure? I mean didn't you plan that trip with the guys for a while?"

"Nothing is more important than you. And yes I am sure."

Erin sat down her fork. "Any idea where?"

"How about the state park we used to visit? We haven't been there in a long time."

Erin's eyes widened. It was where he proposed, and she had tried to get him to go back. But he always had work or something that the guys were doing. "Yes that would be fine. I would like to see the place again."

"Great! Don't you worry about a thing. I will pack the basket." Jack said as he picked up the plates and put them in the sink.

"Jack, are you feeling okay?"

"Never better."

Erin stood and walked over to him, then looked into his eyes. "Are you sure? I mean you don't normally–"

"Erin look, the other night I realized that I haven't been the husband you wanted. I know I haven't been bad, but I haven't been that good either and I am trying to make up for it. Okay?"

"Okay, but at least let me wash the dishes. You did breakfast after all."

Jack laughed and stood aside. "Deal, but I still want to pack the picnic basket."

Erin rinsed a plate off and smiled. "I don't even know where it is."

"Oh, but I do."

Erin turned quickly with her eyes wide. "You do?"

"Sure, don't you remember we put it in the back corner of the garage? It is under a tarp I threw in the corner, that is why you haven't seen it. Sorry about hiding it with the tarp, I was in a hurry but I will make sure to fold it next time."

Erin could not believe what she was hearing. Not only did he want to take her on a picnic, something they hadn't done in many years, but also knew where the basket was when she didn't. Granted, he was in the garage more than her, but to remember so well something that hadn't been used in years?

She forced a smile as she put the last dish in the strainer. "Glad you do, I had no clue."

"Now you can go upstairs and I will get everything ready."

"Upstairs? What for?"

Jack nudged her with his elbow. "To change of course. I thought you might like to for our date."

Erin fought the urge and managed to keep her mouth from hanging open. They hadn't went out on a date in years. While they did a lot together, Jack hadn't used the 'D' word since they got married. It was something else she wanted back. And now here it was, on a sliver platter. She smiled and headed for the stairs. "Oh sure. Won't be but a minute."

Jack grinned. "Of that I am sure."

Erin returned a few minutes later wearing a clingy white flower print dress that rested two inches above her knees, and wedge sandals. But she stopped when she saw Jack had changed as well. Gone were the jeans, replaced by a nice pair of dark pants and a striped polo. He placed several items into the basket on the table and smiled. "You look great love. Ready?"

Erin blinked. "How did you change and make lunch?" She stepped into the kitchen and detected a faint hint of sulfur. "Did you burn something?"

Jack smiled. "My secret, and no I didn't burn anything."

Erin sniffed the air again. "Hmm odd, I thought I smelled something for a minute."

Jack shrugged. "Must have been the food." He winked. "I know I didn't do a stinker."

Erin smiled and wrapped her arms around his muscular torso. "I didn't say you did." She kissed him. "I'm ready."

Jack flipped the basket's lid shut and picked it up. He pointed towards the door. "Then shall we?"

Erin looped her arm through his. "That we shall."

— 4 —

The drive took over an hour with Jack holding Erin's hand the whole way, only letting go to make large turns. They chatted pleasantly about his business, what he and the guys were planning, but he wanted to be with her instead. She caught him looking at her legs more than once and her heart skipped a beat every time.

She always wanted him to notice her more. Sure he did it when they were dating, but after their marriage it quickly faded. He still did on occasion, but those had become few and far between. Granted he had been busy trying to expand the business. But 'us' time had dwindled. Erin had hoped that it would be different once this vacation started, but instead he went out with the guys or something off by himself.

Now here he was dumping the guys to take her on a picnic, looking at her, and holding her hand as if they were still dating. Every time he squeezed her hand, a tingle went through her. She hadn't felt that in a long time.

Jack pulled into the parking lot. The park had changed little since last they saw it. The hills and trees made reflections on the lake that rippled when the wind blew. It was like something out of a picture book. "I'll get the basket. You find us a spot." He said hopping out of the truck.

"Okay." Erin said as she climbed out of the truck. Well that felt like the old Jack. Back when they were dating, he would always help her out of the truck. She stood and watched as he opened the back tool compartment and pulled out their basket.

Jack looked at her. "I thought you were going to find a spot?"

"I thought we could do it together?"

Jack laughed. "Of course love." He walked over and took her hand. "Where to?"

"I think I saw several places along the lake," she said pointing.

Jack smiled. "Then that is where we will go." They walked up to a vacant table near the water. "How about this?"

"Well I was thinking about under that big tree over there." Erin pointed to a large oak tree with lush grass under it. "Oh, I bet you didn't bring a blanket."

Jack smiled. "Actually, yes I did."

Erin stared at him. "You did?"

"Sure. Do you think I would forget one when that is how I proposed?"

"No I didn't." Although she really did.

They walked over to the tree and Jack pulled a large white and red check blanket out of the basket and laid it on the ground. Erin's eyebrow went up momentarily as they didn't have a blanket like that.

She sat down and Jack started getting items out of the basket. A moment later the blanket was full with salads, sandwiches, and even a bag of cookies. "How did you do all of this so fast? And you don't cook!"

Jack laughed. "Hey! I cook some. And it is not as much as you think. The sandwiches are the steaks from the dinner last night I missed, the cookies you made as well. Which, by the way, are wonderful. I couldn't help but sneak one earlier."

Erin smiled. "That's all right. I am glad you like them."

Jack's eyes went wide. "Like them? They are a slice of heaven!" He sat down next to the tree and pulled Erin alongside. He nibbled her ear. "I really am sorry about yesterday. I won't do it again."

Erin smiled and snuggled up under his arm. She ran her fingertips down his shirt while she put her head on his chest. "It's okay. But I found you gone when I woke up, your phone left on the desk, and no word all day long I–"

"I know love, I know. And I am sorry, please forgive me?"

She looked up into his eyes. "I forgive you. But if you ever do that again I am going to kick your backside twice around the planet!"

Jack chuckled. "Got it love, I got it."

"You'd better."

"Shall we eat our lunch?"

Erin smiled. "You bet."

Jack grabbed a sandwich with his free hand and gave it to Erin, then grabbed another for himself. The weather was beautiful, but surprisingly not many people were around. After lunch Jack gave her a squeeze and gazed into her eyes. "What shall we do now?"

She snuggled down and put her head back on his chest. "I am good. We haven't done anything like this in so long, and I am savoring the moment."

Jack kissed her head. "I know, and I will do better. From now on. I promise. Still, we haven't done a lot of things they have here now. Like that paddle boat I see out in the middle of the lake." Jack pointed to a foot-powered boat making its way across the glassy surface of the lake.

Erin looked up. "No we haven't."

"Want to?"

She sat up. "Okay. But if you push me in the lake, you are in deep trouble."

Jack laughed. "Love, I just got you to forgive me. There is no way I am going to ruin that so soon!"

Erin chuckled. "Smart." They walked over to the dock and rented a paddle boat. The boats were a bit expensive per hour, but Jack didn't even flinch and rented one for the whole day. "The whole day? Are we going to paddle around all day?"

"No, but I didn't want us to run out of time either." Jacked helped Erin into the little boat and the foot-driven peddles in the base drove a propeller in back. One couldn't race around in it without exhausting themselves, but for a slow relaxed ride it was very efficient and enjoyable.

They paddled up and down the lake noting the many campers nestled along its banks on the other side of the lake. Nether noticed a little plug in the back of the boat had opened. When they stopped to look at a crane that had landed in the distance, Erin took her feet off the pedals placing them on the floor of the boat. Her eyes went wide when they touched cold water. "Jack! We are sinking!"

Jack looked down and saw the water building in the footwells. "What? How?" His head moved in a blur of motion until he noticed a small drain plug in the back between them. "I see a drain plug, the seal must have given way." He reached behind but couldn't quite touch it. "I can't reach it. And if I move so I can, it will capsize us. Back do the dock! It is all we can do." They peddled as fast as they could, but the boat had slowed down with all the extra water that continued to pour in.

"I don't think we are going to make it."

"We can and will. Pedal!"

They pedaled faster, but it didn't seem to change their speed. By now the water was high enough that their feet were under water and slowing them down even further.

Erin shivered. "Dang this water is cold!"

"Keep peddling!"

They were a few yards from the dock when the water lapped over the side and the boat started to slip under the water. A second later they were swimming as the boat sunk to the bottom. "Jack! My leg! I can't ..." She sank beneath the water.

"Erin!" Jack dove under the water. She was sinking fast. He swam like a fish, grabbed and hauled her to the surface. She coughed as she gulped in fresh air. He pulled her to the dock and pushed her up over the old boards. "You okay?" he said between deep breaths.

Erin coughed again. "Yes I am fine. That water is like ice though. How did you manage to swim so well?"

Jack smiled. "With the thought of losing you, how could I not?"

The attendant peered up from his e-reader in time to see them pop out of the water onto the dock. He ran out of the shed. "Are you folks okay?"

Jack's eyes grew fire red. "We are. No thanks to you!"

The man blinked. "Me? What did I do?"

"You are in charge of the maintenance of these boats, are you not?"

"Ye ... yes."

"Well then, how do you think the state will react when they find out my wife almost died due to a fault in a water craft you maintained!"

"Sir ... I–"

"Jack, it was an accident."

Jack's glare didn't waver. If looks could kill, the man would have been incinerated on the spot. "A very preventable one."

"Sir, here is your money back, and then some." The man pressed a wad of cash into Jack's hand. "Please, we never had anything happen like this before. And you can be sure it won't happen again."

Erin took Jack's other hand and smiled. "Jack, I am fine. Really, I am. Let's go home and forget this."

He gazed into her eyes and smiled, then turned his head back to the man. "All right, consider yourself lucky."

"Thank you sir," he said running back to the shed. A moment later he reappeared with a blanket. "Here. Wrap your wife in this and take her home. Don't worry about bringing the blanket back. Keep it with my compliments."

"Thank you." Jack wrapped the blanket around Erin and squeezed her. "Let's go home love." They went back to the picnic area to collect their basket and headed for the truck. But before they got there, an announcement came over the various loudspeakers.

"All water craft please return to the dock immediately! Your money will be refunded. I say again, all water craft return to the dock immediately!"

Jack snorted. "Well better late than never."

Erin shivered under the blanket. "At least they are trying."

He snorted again. "If you say so."

They reached the truck, he helped Erin in, placed the basket in the back, and headed out of the parking lot. He turned the heat up to max in the already warm interior.

"Jack, I am fine. You don't need to worry. And what are you trying to do? Bake me? I am not a cake you know."

He looked over and saw she was no longer shivering. He

gripped her hand which felt warm in his grasp. "Sorry love, I wanted to get you dry."

"You are going to cook me instead." She reached over and flipped off the heat. Sitting back she regarded Jack, who wasn't even sweating.

He blew out a breath. "Well so much for our date."

"Well, it was memorable."

Jack laughed. "Yeah, but not in a good way."

"Oh I don't know. I got to spend a lovely picnic with my husband, then took a bath with him."

Jack threw back his head and laughed. "Oh I love you."

"And I love you. But next time you want to take a bath with me, just ask. And let's do it at home in a nice warm tub?"

Jack grinned and squeezed her hand. "Deal."

Erin rolled over to see Jack's smiling face. "Hello beautiful. Sleep well?"

She leaned over and kissed him. "You know I did. Thank you for the wonderful day yesterday."

Jack reached over and pulled her close. "I don't think it was that good. And I intend on making it up to you today."

"You don't need to. It was a lovely day *and* night."

"One where you took a cold bath in a lake and almost drown."

Erin smiled. "But you didn't let that happen. So don't worry about it. Deal?"

Jack sighed and squeezed her tighter. "Deal. But I am still going to cook you breakfast and then we can go."

Erin blinked. "Go? Go where?"

"That's a surprise."

"Another surprise?" Erin said sitting up.

Jack's grin was wide enough to drive a truck through. "Yes."

"Any hints?"

"Nope."

"Aw, you are no fun."

"Oh to the contrary, I think this is."

"Oh hush you!" She kissed him deeply before he could say another word. When she came up for air, he only grinned. "Still no hint?"

Jack shook his head rolling it back and forth on the pillow. "Nope. Nothing you can say will make me tell either."

Erin grinned. "Say perhaps, but I have other ways of making you talk."

"Uh oh."

"Yeah, care to revise that statement Mr. Winecker?"

"Ummm ..."

Erin folded her arms over her naked breasts. "I'm waiting."

"Ummm ... no comment."

"Okay, you asked for it Mr. Winecker." She reached down under the sheet and found what she was aiming for. She caressed in a certain spot and his body responded immediately tenting the sheet.

"Oh gosh not there! We don't have time for this!" Erin caressed further. "Erin!!"

"Yes we do, or is there something you want to tell me?"

Jack bit his tongue. "Er ... no."

"Okayyy you asked for it." She caressed a several more times then pulled down the sheet and straddled him. She began to lower herself.

Jack sucked in a breath. "Wait! You win! But you do realize that if we weren't pressed for time, I wouldn't have given in."

Erin grinned playing with his chest. "I know." She got on all fours above him and peered into his eyes. "Now spill it! Or we are going to be very late for something."

"Top Point! I planned to take you to Top Point today."

Erin raised an eyebrow. "The amusement park?"

Jack nodded then reached up placing both hands on her

naked waist. "Yes, we haven't been there in years. And we used to have a lot of fun there back when were first dating."

"It's over three hours away. Are you sure? We could do something closer."

"Yes I am sure. Unless, you don't want to."

"No, not at all. I would love to go, just making sure you wanted to."

"I wouldn't have planned the surprise if I didn't want to."

"Yeah I know, but I have asked in the past and you always said it was too far."

"That was then, this is now. Besides, I am trying to make it up to you for yesterday. Now would you mind putting those weapons away?" Jack waved a finger towards her naked breasts then pointed to the area between her hips.

"Sure thing." She leaned back and started to sit down again. His body immediately rose to the occasion.

"No! We don't–"

Erin bent forward and kissed him. "You are so easy." She hopped off, picked up the panties laying on the floor from yesterday, and slipped them on. "There, my weapon is put away."

Jack swung his legs over and stood up. "Well one is, two are still out," he said with a wink.

Erin took a step forward and her breasts squished up against his chest as she wrapped her arms around him. "I will put them away after my shower. Deal?"

Jack squeezed her tightly. "Deal my darling. I will cook us breakfast while you do."

"You sure? You cooked breakfast yesterday."

"Yeah, I did. But I also have years of breakfasts that you made and I never even said thank you for."

"Oh I know you were thankful, just busy at the time. I understand about your job. It is not easy running a business."

Jack squeezed her again. "How did I ever manage to end up with such a wonderful woman as you?" At those words Erin's knees went weak. If she wasn't holding on to Jack, she might have gone down in a heap.

"Just lucky I guess." She kissed him.

"Luckiest guy in the world then." He kissed her back. "I am off to the kitchen or we will never make it to Top Point." He turned to leave but Erin slapped him playfully on the backside. "What was that for?"

"Aren't you forgetting something?"

Jack looked off into space for a minute then turned back to Erin. "No, I don't think so."

"You might want these," she said throwing underwear and a pair of pants at him which he caught in the air. "I don't particularly want all the neighborhood women drooling over you through the open blinds."

"Oh! Right!" He slipped them on and headed out the door.

Erin slipped off her panties, threw them into the hamper, and climbed into the shower. Her body ached like the previous morning and set the shower massager to full force. "Well at least I don't have to worry about gaining weight right now."

She climbed out, toweled off, hung it over the bar, and dried her hair. When it was dry, she walked out of the bathroom and over to her dresser. She grabbed a set of white underwear, a dark green t-shirt that matched her eyes, a pair of jeans, slid them on, then went downstairs.

She found Jack sitting at the table with his usual grin as of late. Her eyebrow rose when she saw he was now wearing a pair of black jeans and a dark blue t-shirt. The air had a faint hint of sulfur. "Well look who decided to come downstairs."

"Oh hush you. You know we women take longer."

Jack stood up, leaned over, and kissed her. "I know it. And you are always worth the wait." He eyed her up and down then licked his lips. "Mmmmmm, if we didn't have plans, I would be taking you back upstairs right now."

Erin's leaned on the chair in front of her for support as her knees buckled from the thoughts of the previous nights. She yanked her mind to the present and noticed the table. Jack had went all out with toast cut diagonal, buttered, and a large cheese omelet with bacon. She thought about her diet, then tossed it to the wind. "Wow this looks good."

"I hope it tastes good too." Jack pulled the chair out in front of Erin and gestured to it. "For you Mrs. Winecker."

"Thank you Mr. Winecker." Erin said as he pushed her in causing the chair to make a slight squeaking sound.

After eating, Jack picked up the plates and started washing them in the sink. Erin's mouth fell open, and she snapped it shut before he could notice. "Clean up too? I can do that."

Jack shrugged. "Why? I made the mess, it is only fitting that I clean up."

"But you made it for me."

"And you have done it countless times, and I never hopped up and said 'Let me help you with that.' did I?"

Erin shuffled her white sneakered feet. "No, but–"

Jack continued washing the dish and placed it in the drying rack. "Then I rest my case. Besides, this will only take a minute."

Erin shrugged. "I will grab my purse." When she returned two minutes later, Jack stood there waiting. "Done already?"

"Yes I told you it would only take a minute."

"I know, but I didn't think you meant it literally. I have been doing it for years, and I am not that fast. You must tell me your secret."

Jack stepped forward and kissed her on the cheek. "Maybe someday." He took her hand and squeezed it. "Shall we?"

"Lead the way Mr. Winecker."

The drive to Top Point was uneventful, but enjoyable. Jack talked about work and the upgrades going on at the sawmill. What some of the guys were up to. She wondered what happened to Jack that changed him so much. He didn't used to talk this much about the guys or work. Granted he thought it would bore her, but to the contrary, she always wanted to know about his life. She also ached for so long to be more a part of it. Now here he was doing exactly that, and she didn't know what to make of it.

"So what do you think?"

Erin blinked. "Hmm?"

"Earth to Erin ... Earth to Erin come in Erin."

She slapped him playfully. "Will you stop!"

"So where were you?"

"Huh?"

"Well you weren't here with me, that is for sure. You looked like you were million miles away."

"Oh. I was thinking about a dress Jane was working on. That's all," she lied.

"Hmm, here I am talking about the guys and if I should go with them to the big game next week, and you are thinking about dresses? I didn't know I was that boring."

She grabbed his hand and squeezed. "You aren't! You get that thought out of your head this instant. I love it when you talk to me. Please don't ever stop."

Jack laughed. "Okay, you convinced me. You know I never could resist that look."

Erin's face cracked into a lopsided grin. "What look?"

Jack laughed. "And there is another one. Geez, you have a bigger arsenal than our country does of nuclear weapons!"

"Only for you my darling."

"Good thing. Ah here is our exit." Jack said as he turned the wheel. A few minutes later they were driving in an ocean of parked cars. "See a spot?"

"Yes, I think I see one in the next row over," Erin said pointing.

"Ah, I see it." Jack guided the truck into the narrow space. They walked to the front gate and Jack pulled out his wallet. Erin gulped when the price was quoted, but Jack didn't even flinch. He even paid extra for the VIP passes and gave one to Erin.

"Be sure to wear that all times." The man in the ticket booth said pointing to the passes. "They allow you to access the express lines or jump to the front of others if there isn't one. They also will get you two free meals. Simply have the cashier scan the pass."

Jack nodded. "Thank you. Have a good day."

"You too, sir."

Erin pulled him away and whispered. "How much did you spend on these things?! I didn't even know they had VIP here."

"Neither did I, but when I saw the perks, I couldn't resist. We will make good use of them today."

"But–"

"Erin, I told you before, this is my treat. Don't worry about it. And before you ask, yes the mill is doing well. It is not going under. This is not a last hurrah. I am trying to make it up to you for yesterday. Will you please let me?"

Erin sighed. "Sorry, I guess I am not used to you spending money like that's all."

Jack's eyebrow raised. "Am I that bad?"

"Let's just say that you could give Scrooge a tip or two."

"I am not that bad."

"True, you are worse," Erin said with a smile.

Jack squeezed her hand. "You are going to get it."

"Promises, promises."

"Nope, that's a guarantee. Once I get you home that is." Jack winked.

Erin's grin widened. "I am looking forward to it. Now which ride shall we do first?"

"How about the teacup?" Jack pointed to the teacups spinning around on a raised platform a few yards away.

Erin's eyebrows met. "Teacups? I thought you might want to ride The Warp." She pointed to the large roller coaster on the other side of the park.

"Well I know coasters are not your thing," Jack chuckled.

"True, teacups it is."

They stood in line but as soon as the operator saw the passes hanging from their belt loops, he motioned them to come to the front of the line. The ride stopped a moment later, and they hopped into one of the large tea cups and shut the door. Erin slid up next to Jack, and he put his arm around her. The cups started up, and they spun around the floor with increasing speed. Erin held onto Jack. They watched the world spin around them and smiled.

When the ride stopped, Erin stood up then fell backward into Jack's lap. "I told you, not until we get back home." He winked.

"Very funny. I lost my balance for a second is all." She stuck her tongue out.

"Careful Mrs. Winecker. Them's fightn' words. I might make use of that tongue." He said closing the distance between her face and his.

She hopped up and left the tea cup before he could. "Oh you are going to get it."

Jack grinned as he stood up. "Promises, promises."

"Oh you will, trust me. Now where to next?"

"Up to you my love. I drove us here, now it is your turn."

"Hmm, how about that Haunted House ride? If they still have it?"

Jack nodded. "Sure, that will be fun."

They wandered around, and after a bit found the Haunted House. The line was huge going around the building. But once again their passes came in handy. They were in the little car heading inside the Haunted House in less than five minutes. "I have to admit, those passes were a good idea."

Jack leaned forward. "What's that? I couldn't hear you. I thought you said I was right."

She slapped him playfully. "Oh hush you."

"Maybe."

After the large double doors snapped shut behind them, various realistic projections of creatures appeared. One even shot into their little car. Erin forgot about that and she jumped into Jack's lap and threw her arms around him. He could feel her heart pounding next to his. "Hmmm I am going to have to remember this ride, and come here more often," he said with a sly smile.

Erin squeezed him then laughed. "Oh I love you."

He gave her a squeeze back. "Ditto."

They rode all different kinds of rides throughout the day.

Some were fast, others were more like attending a show with special effects than a ride. For lunch they decided on tacos, and while included with their tickets, Jack paid anyway. Erin's eyebrow went up, and she tilted her head but didn't say anything until they sat down. "Why didn't you want to use the pass?"

"Because I don't think that vendor is included in the deal. Besides, he has a family of four to feed."

Erin's eyes went wide as she leaned forward. "How do you know that?"

"Remember when you went to look for napkins? He pointed to the extra cheese on my taco and said his kids did the same thing. All four of them."

Erin nodded as she bit into her taco, but wondered as she didn't recall them having a conversation. Granted it was noisy, but she wasn't that far away. She swallowed and wiped some sauce from her chin. "What would you like to do next?"

"I told you, you are driving. You tell me." Jack grinned, then took another bite from his taco.

Erin shook her head. "Nope you have let me pick all this time. Now it is your turn."

Jack swallowed. "Nope."

"Okay then, The Warp it is!"

"What?!" Jack sputtered sending two bits of taco that landed on his paper plate.

"You heard me. Don't think that I haven't noticed the looks you keep giving it. It's the only thing in this park that gets that look, except me!"

"Well ..." Jack looked down at his plate and moved it around with a finger. "I do admit, I would like to ride it someday. I mean, it has the latest in linear induction technology. You don't get drawn up by a chain to a high peak, then dropped. It blasts you out of the gate! That must be wild!"

With Jack's enthusiasm for the ride, and that he was willing to put it off for her, only made her smile grow. "I'm sure."

Jack took her hand into his and squeezed. "Are you sure? I mean, I know coasters are not your thing."

Erin nodded. "Yes I am sure. And if you think you are going on it, without me, you have another thing coming!"

"But I was just thinking–"

"I know what you were thinking, and while I could wait on the sidelines. I will not be thought of as the wimpy wife that waited on the side while her husband rode The Warp."

Jack grinned. "But no one would ever–"

"Uh-huh, I can see the watercooler conversation at the sawmill now. No way!"

"I wouldn't–"

She leaned forward and kissed his lips tasting a speck of sauce he missed. "I know you wouldn't. But I couldn't help teasing. However, I'm still riding with you."

Jacked watched her unwavering gaze, and he sighed. "Guess I am not going to win this am I?"

"Nope." Erin popped the last of the taco into her mouth and munched. "Not a chance."

Jack stood up, picked up their plates and threw it into the trash. "Let's head over. I am sure there is a long line."

She looped her arm into his. "Right with you."

The line reached around the main entrance three times. Even with their passes, the wait was over fifteen minutes before one of the small two seater trains were available. They climbed in, the attendant lowered the shoulder harness, and locked them into place. "Please remember to keep your hands inside the vehicle at all times." They nodded and he returned to the control booth. A voice boomed over several loud speakers. "You are about to enter The Warp. Prepare for launch ...5 ...4 ..."

Jack grabbed Erin's hand and squeezed. "This is going to be fun."

Erin swallowed hard. "Yeah right."

"3 ...2 ...1 ...LAUCH!" Powerful, unseen, linear induction motors powered up, and they were shoved back into their seats as the small craft shot out of the gate like a cannon ball. The craft curved as it followed the track, then spun several times entering a corkscrew.

"Yeah-hooo!"

Erin shut her eyes. "Just tell me when it is over!" The train continued on spinning, throwing them upside down, then back again in an eye blink. "Ohh I wish I didn't eat that taco!" Two minutes later they were slowing down and heading back into the building from the opposite side. But suddenly, instead of braking, the induction motors kicked in accelerating them at top speed. It shot them back out of the building before the operator could blink. With the added inertia, the train hit a sharp turn at speeds far beyond what the designers has intended. It jumped the track and went hurtling towards a brick wall at the start of The Warp enclosure.

"Jack!" Erin screamed and shut her eyes again.

They hit with a loud bang and the car crumpled. The smell of sulfur stung Erin's nose as bricks and mortar rained down around them. When the dust settled, Erin opened her eyes. The train's front had crumpled, but stopped a nanometer short of touching them. She looked over at Jack. His face was ashen as he turned towards her. "Are you okay? Please be okay."

Erin coughed. "I am okay. What a ride!"

Jack threw back his head and laughed. "Oh what a wife I have! I love you."

The attendant ran over to them. "Sir! Ma'am! Are you hurt? I don't know what the heck happened. I hit the brakes, not the accelerator. And there are three safeties that are supposed to stop that from ever happening. I hit the emergency call. The park doctor will be here in a minute."

Jack stood up brushing the brick dust from his shirt, then helped Erin up. "We are fine. The doctor is not needed, thank you anyway."

The attended shuddered. "Sir, I would feel better if you got checked out."

Erin coughed. "We are fine. We don't need anything other than a shower."

"Still, we would appreciate it if you would let our doctor make sure." They turned to see a man in a suit walking towards them. "I am Gilbart Goddard. You call me GG. I own this establishment."

Jack helped Erin out of what was left of the train, over the mess of bricks, brushed the dust from his hands and reached out for the man's hand. "Nice to meet you GG, we have been coming here for years."

GG looked down at the still grubby hand, sighed, put on a smile, and grabbed it. "Always nice to meet our repeat customers. I do not know how this happened, but you can rest assured we will get to the bottom of it." Releasing Jack's hand he turned towards the attendant. "Close the ride until a full investigation is done. I will not risk anyone else. Is that clear?"

The attendant nodded. "Yes, Boss." He turned and walked back to the control booth. Upon entering he picked up a microphone and flipped several switches. Loud feedback could be heard on speakers all over the park. "To all visitors, we regret to inform you The Warp is now closed for maintenance. We will announce when it reopens."

GG wiped his hand with a handkerchief. "Again please accept my apologies. I am very surprised you were not injured, are you sure you will not accept an examination from our doctor?"

Jack nodded. "I am sure. We are fine, thank you for your concern."

"Well then, would you at least accompany me back to the office? I would like you sign a release that we offered medical assistance, but you refused. Otherwise, the legality of the situation could escalate."

Erin frowned. "We are not going to sue you, it was an accident."

"Still, I appreciate signing the release. I will make it worth your while."

Jack's eyebrow went up. "Oh?"

GG leaned closer. "How does free VIP lifetime passes sound?"

"You've got a deal," Jack said smiling.

As they walked towards the office, Erin glanced back at the disaster that used to be a roller coaster car. The front was bashed in, the seats pushed up, the wheels were missing, and the back crumpled almost as bad the nose. It looked like a large soda can after a giant hand drained it, then crushed it in a show of strength. How did they survive? The only part intact was their seats. Erin's thoughts were still whirling when they reached the office.

GG reached inside a file cabinet and pulled out two sheets

of paper. "Here we are, two 1084B forms. Just fill in your name, address, and sign the bottom."

Jack scrutinized the short paperwork. "You are right, it only states we refused medical examination. However, this one part at the bottom could be interpreted to waving the right of a lawsuit should we choose in the future."

GG's face hardened. "Is that a problem?"

Jack shook his head. "Nope. We are fine, no harm done. That is all I care about. Besides, I am not going to turn down a lifetime pass."

Erin nodded. "Agreed." She signed her form as Jack did the same.

GG smiled. "Thank you." He walked over, placed both inside a copy machine, then handed them the copies. "There you are, and I will get your lifetime passes." He bent down and opened a lower drawer of his desk with a key, then pulled out two golden plastic tags, and handed them over. "These will give you the same express access, and then some. It will also give you access to areas not normally open to the public, if you want. If you ever lose them, just see me for a new set. They are active now, you can use them today if you wish."

"Thank you," Jack said taking them. "But I think we have had enough excitement for one day. I need to take my wife home."

Erin nodded. "Yes and I need a shower."

GG smiled again. "Very well. I hope to see you again real soon."

Jack raised the hand holding the new passes in a salute motion. "I am sure you will."

The ride back home was quieter. But Jack did ask repeatedly if she was okay. "I told you I am fine. I just need a shower. Stop worrying."

"Sorry love, I can't help it," Jack said squeezing her hand.

Erin watched the landscape slide pass the window. Two accidents in two days was too much. But lightning can strike twice. Unlikely, but not impossible. And how had they survived? Unless probability had gone out the window, something was going on. She shoved the thoughts out of her mind as Jack returned to talking about the activity at work.

— 6 —

Light poured through the window and Erin opened an eye. Before she could turn an arm came around from behind, pulled her close and Jack nibbled her ear. "Good morning my precious."

She turned and ran her fingers down the side of his face, feeling his morning stubble. "I'm your precious now, eh? I am fine with that unless you change your name to Gollum. Then we might have a problem." She winked.

Jack chuckled and squeezed her tight. "I am not Gollum. However, you are more precious to me than the ring was to him."

Erin melted into his arms. "Ohhh if you keep saying things like that, we won't be leaving this bed all day."

Jack grinned. "Promise?"

She squeezed him hard. "You bet."

"Mmmmm, it is tempting, but we do need to eat, and I was thinking perhaps that little place in town–"

Erin sat up. "You have another *date* planned for today?"

Jack looked away. "Yeah, I do. The last two didn't work out so well, I am hoping that third times the charm."

"You have got to be kidding. They were lovely times, even with the unexpected moments."

"Ha! That is one nice way to put it. If our original dates went anything like those, you would have never said 'yes'."

Erin laughed. "You are probably right. But I hope I would realize what a catch you are."

Jack's eyebrow rose. "Me? I don't know about that. You on the other hand–"

Erin hit him with a pillow. "You are and you know it. How about we stay here today instead?"

"Well, I made reservations."

"You did? Where?"

"Le Bloch's," Jack said sitting up.

Erin blinked. "Le Bloch's? They charge an arm and a leg. Not to mention it is almost impossible to get a reservation."

"The key word here is *'almost'*." Jack's grin returned wider than before.

"How did you ever manage it?"

"That's a secret."

"Uh-huh." Erin pushed him back down, straddled him on all fours. "Now are you going to talk, or do I need to use my weapons again?"

"Err well ..."

She leaned down, kissed his lips, then started lowering her hips. His body started to respond, almost touching her, and she went down a micron more. "Stop! You win! One, it is for lunch. Two, lunch reservations are much less crowded. And three, I have a buddy that owned me a favor."

"A buddy, huh? I guess I can believe that. Knowing how irresistible you are." She bent back down, kissed his lips, then rolled off. "Well I guess I had better get started if we are going to Le Bloch's." She couldn't believe this. Jack had made excuses for years and now he was not only offering, he had called in a favor to do it.

Jack blinked. "Get started?"

Erin rolled her eyes. "You know we women take longer than you to get ready. And if we are going to Le Bloch's, you had better believe that I am not going in jeans and a t-shirt!"

"No, of course not but–"

"No buts. Now shoo! I have a lot of work to do." Erin pulled him out of bed and pushed him towards the door.

"But this is my room too you know."

"Not for the next few hours it isn't. Now get." She hustled him out of the room, shut the door and leaned up against it. A knock jarred her out of her thoughts.

"Erin? Umm . . . I do need some clothes."

Erin walked over to the pile from the previous day, picked them up, opened the door a crack, and threw them in his face. "There you are, now scoot!"

The door shut in his face. "If I had known this was going to kick me out of my own bedroom, I would have had second thoughts!" he shouted through the door.

A muffled reply came back. "Oh hush! You will like the result."

"Yeah, but at this moment I am not sure it is worth it." He grumbled as he pulled on his boxers and jeans, then went downstairs to make breakfast. After it was done, he sat everything on the kitchen table and waited. The food started to get cold, and he went back upstairs to see what the problem was. He knocked on the door. "Erin? Are you all right?"

"Yes? Why?" A muffled voice responded.

"Because your breakfast is getting cold."

"I told you I have a lot to do. I don't have time. I will eat later at Le Bloch's."

"But–"

"I am fine. I will eat later."

Jack sighed. "I think you should eat something, but if you are sure ..." He trailed off then knocked on the door again. "You know I need to get in there too."

The door opened a crack, and a hand appeared holding a garment bag. Jack took it as his eyebrows met. "What's this?" He unzipped the bag and found his black suit, shirt, and tie. In the bottom of the bag, laid his dress shoes. Jack grunted. "Fine! But I still need a shower you know," he shouted through the door.

"Use the bathroom in the hall."

"But my soap and stuff is in ours."

"Check the zippered pouch on the bag."

Jack unzipped it and found his shampoo, soap, toothbrush and toothpaste. "Geez, I am banished to the hall? She must be more mad than I thought."

"What was that?" A muffled voice called.

"*Nothing*. Going to take my shower." Jack went into the hall bathroom, hung up the bag, and went back downstairs to put the remnants of breakfast away. A few minutes later he was back upstairs and in the shower. Twenty minutes after that he was wearing a hole in the living room carpet, pacing back and forth. He kept checking his watch getting more anxious by the minute. When the clock showed they had less than an hour left Jack walked back upstairs and knocked on the door.

"Erin? Are you ready yet? We have to leave soon if we want to make our reservations."

"Just about ... one minute."

"Better be a fast minute," Jack grumbled.

"You can come in now."

Jack gripped the doorknob, turned it and pushed open the door. "About time! We need to–" His mouth dropped. Erin stood there in a shiny black cocktail dress with a deep scoop neck. Her long black hair was feathered and curled framing her face perfectly. And the makeup on her face made his eyes pop. When he could get his eyes to move again, they drifted down her long legs encased in conforming sheer black nylon, ending in a pair of black leather four inch pumps.

She licked her red glossy lips and put a hand to her pearl necklace. "Well?"

"Wow!"

Erin smiled. "I take it you approve?"

"Approve? Approve? Gosh that is the understatement of the year. No, century!"

Erin's smile broadened. "Good. Worth the wait then?"

Jack stood there for a minute before realizing she said something. "Oh heck yeah!"

She walked over to him, hearing the click-click of her heels echoing around the room. She looped her arm through his. "Well then Mr. Winecker, shall we go eat?"

"Definitely." He leaned close and kissed her on the cheek.

"Careful. Don't mess my makeup."

"I was. You didn't really think I would mess that up did you? We wouldn't get out of here before dark if I did."

She playfully punched him in the side. "Ha-ha, very funny Mr. Winecker."

Jack laughed. "I thought it was."

They walked out of the house and Erin started towards the truck when Jack stopped her. "I thought you were in a hurry?"

"I am."

"Well then how are we going to get to Le Bloch's? I am certainly not walking there!"

"Of course not," Jack chuckled. "But our ride will be here in a minute."

Erin's eyebrow rose. "Our ride?" She gazed down the road and saw a white shape approaching. When it pulled up, she realized it was a white limousine. "A limo? Are you kidding?"

"Nope." He walked over, opened the door, and gestured to the seat. "For you Mrs. Winecker."

"This day is full of surprises." She slid into the plush seat and swung her legs in.

Jack shut the door, walked to the other side, and hopped in. He hit the intercom button. "Le Bloch's, most direct route please."

"Yes sir." The driver said before the intercom clicked off. A moment later they were riding down the road and Erin could only think it was true about limos. They did ride like a dream. But at that moment, she wasn't sure if this was a dream or not.

The limo pulled up to Le Bloch's, and the driver helped Erin out of the car as Jack walked around from the other side. There were more than a few glances when the limo drove up. Jack extended his arm. "Ready Mrs. Winecker?"

She looped her arm around his. "Definitely Mr. Winecker."

The driver shut the door and began walking to the other side. "Please park the car and be ready to take us to another location. I will call when we are finished here," Jack said over his shoulder.

The man inclined his head. "Yes sir." He climbed inside and drove away.

They walked inside the lush restaurant that was Le Bloch's. The mahogany paneling had gold inserts of the restaurant's symbolic willow tree giving the whole room a feeling of class that could not be beat. Erin could feel the plush red carpet through her shoes as they entered. A man wearing a black tux behind a podium looked up. "Welcome to Le Bloch's, do you have a reservation?"

Jack nodded. "We do indeed. Mr. and Mrs. Winecker."

The man scanned the tablet screen sitting on his podium. "Ah yes, here it is. We have a table in one of the private rooms ready for you, if you will follow me please."

They nodded and followed the man through the entrance, into the main dinning room. Erin stopped. The room reeked of elegance with its flickering lights on the walls and perfectly set tables with detailed table cloths. The ceiling contained a skylight covered in stained glass. And while there was plenty of light, each table had a lit candle. There wasn't an empty table in the whole room. Jack whispered. "Erin, don't worry, we have a table. He even said so."

"I know, but wow this place is more than I dreamed. Are you sure we can afford it?"

"Will you stop worrying and come on? He is going to notice."

The man did notice, stopped, and walked back towards them. "Is there a problem Monsieur?"

"Not at all, my wife has not been here before and was looking around. My apologizes, if you would please continue."

"Oh I see Monsieur, it is not a problem. This way Monsieur." The man gestured towards a room off to the side in back. When they entered Erin sucked in a breath. This room was even more luxurious. Paintings adorned the walls, framed by curtains on either side. A smaller stained glass panel rested in the ceiling, and the chair seats were covered in red velvet. The backs and legs had intricate carved images of trees and leaves. The top of the table itself was inlaid with different wood then highlighted in gold in the shape of a large weeping willow. The feet were carved in the same manner as the chairs and ended in claw. A sheer tablecloth did nothing to hide the master craftsmanship underneath.

The man walked over, pulled out a chair, and gestured to it. "Madame?" Erin sat in the chair and he pushed her in. "I shall get your menus, one moment please."

"Are you sure we can afford this? And private dining room?" She said as soon as the man was out of earshot.

Jack leaned close. "I told you not to worry about it, so don't."

"But–"

"Here are your menus." The man said as he placed two folded and leather enclosed items on the table. "A waiter shall be here in a few moments. But if you have any issues, please do let me know." The man inclined his head, turned on his heal, and left.

Erin picked up one of the menus feeling the soft leather and traced her finger along the gold logo of the tree on the front before opening it. "All right, if you are sure, I am not going to say anything more."

"Thank you." He said opening his menu and glancing at the contents. "The Le Coq Au Vin looks good."

Erin looked up and blinked. "The what?"

Jack grinned. "The chicken in red wine sauce."

"Ohh, since when did you learn to speak French?" Erin said as she gazed back down at the menu.

"Since they put the English translation on the other side."

Erin laughed quietly flipping over the page. "I should have known. And that does sound good, perhaps I will just let you order."

Jack grinned. "Are you sure?"

"Well I don't think you can go wrong by looking at the great selection."

Jack's grin widened. "Then I will."

A moment later another man in a tuxedo with a red vest entered the room and bowed slightly. "I am your waiter for the afternoon." He pulled out a pad and flipped back its leather cover. "Are you ready to order?"

Jack nodded. "We are indeed. We will have the Caesar salad, and the Le Coq Au Vin."

The waiter scribbled on his pad. "Excellent choices Monsieur. And the wine?"

"Your best Chardonnay."

Erin gulped.

"And will there be anything else?"

Jack glanced back to the menu. "Hmm, while I know it is not usually available for lunch, how about the Creme Brulee?"

The waiter nodded and scribbled something further on his pad. "I think that can be arranged Monsieur. I shall return in a moment." He took their menus, turned, and left.

Erin's one eyebrow went up. "What was that all about?"

"What do you mean?"

"The bit about dessert?"

"Oh I had heard that we shouldn't leave here without trying their Creme Burlee." Jack shrugged. "That's all."

"Uh-huh, and where did you hear that?"

"I don't remember, does it matter?"

Erin sighed. "I suppose not. But I have wanted to come here for a long time, and I never heard about their Creme Brulee. Heck, I don't even know what it is."

Jack grinned as he took her hand from across the table. "Well then you are in for a treat."

"What? No clues?"

"Nope, nothing you can do will get me to talk either."

Erin's eyebrow went back up. "Oh? So sure of that are you?"

"Here? You bet."

Erin looked around. The room was in the back with its own entrance, no one could see in and the waiter would be a few minutes. She slipped a foot out of her shoe and inched it up his pant leg.

"Erin!" Jack said in a hushed tone. "Not here!"

"What ever are you talking about Mr. Winecker?"

"You know very well what I am–" Erin's foot slid between his legs and felt a tightness growing in the front of his pants. Jack's voice went up an octave even though he was trying to stay quiet. "Erin! Cut it out!"

"I have no idea what you are–"

"You do too! And cut it out!"

"Tell me what I want to know, and perhaps whatever it is you are flustered about will stop."

"All right! It is caramelized vanilla creme with strawberry and black pepper sorbet."

"What are you trying to do? Have me gain ten pounds today?" She wiggled her foot for good measure.

"Erin!"

She pulled her foot back and slipped it back into the waiting pump. "It would have been nice to have been asked."

Jack sighed as his pulse slowed. "But you told me to order–"

"The main course yes, although we had agreed upon the same thing. Nothing was mentioned about dessert. And you know I don't usually eat dessert."

"Yes, I know, but I thought you might want to make an exception since we have never been here before."

"I will. But it still would have been nice to have been asked." Erin sat back. She wasn't really mad at him, but she couldn't let him get away with it either.

"I goofed. I am sorry."

Erin grinned. "Accepted Mr. Winecker. Although, I think you enjoyed my method of getting you to talk."

"Normally yes, not here though!"

Erin was about to say something more when the waiter returned and placed two smallish plates covered in a star pattern of lettuce, Parmesan cheese, croutons, and anchovies, then left. Her nose wrinkled at the anchovies in the center.

"I am sorry, I forgot they were a part of the salad. Put them to the side."

Erin stared at him, frowned, and moved the little things to the side with a sound of disgust. "Ugh I can't imagine how people eat these things."

"They aren't–" Erin glared daggers and Jack cleared this throat. "Yes, well, I am sorry. I promise the rest will make up for it."

Erin sighed. "I know you didn't do it intentionally. Don't worry about it." She munched on several pieces of lettuce and croutons. "The rest is very good though."

A few minutes later, the waiter walked in, saw their silverware placed on the empty plates, removed them, and left. He returned a moment later with their meal and placed it in front of them. "The sommelier will be here in a moment with your wine." Jack nodded, and the man left.

Erin's mouth watered. In the center of the plate two large slices of chicken intersected each other, covered in a red sauce, and elegantly garnished. She couldn't help but pull out her phone to take a picture.

"Erin? What are you doing?"

"I doubt we will be here again anytime soon, so I thought I would take a photo."

A grey-haired man with a tastevin around his neck walked into the room chuckling. "Monsieur, that is fine and quite common. Do not trouble yourself, it is not considered rude here at Le Bloch's." He placed a bottle of wine on the table, produced his knife, flipped out the corkscrew, inserted it into the cork, and extracted it with one deft motion. He removed the cork from the screw and handed it to Jack. "A excellent choice if I may say so, we haven't had anyone request it in a long time."

Jack smiled, inspected the cork in his hand with its deep embossing on the side, and placed it on the table. "I didn't actually request it, only your best chardonnay."

The sommelier leaned closer as he poured the wine into Jack's glass. The liquid's golden tint told its age. "I know Monsieur, but most men in front of a lady try to act as though they did." The man said in a hushed tone.

Jack chuckled. "I can see that. But I have no need to do so in front of my wife."

The man's eyes widened. "That is good to hear."

Erin stared at them as her eyebrow went up. "What are you two talking about?"

The man spoke first as he poured liquid into Erin's glass. "Wine Madame, nothing more."

"And how some people try to be more than they are and get themselves into trouble."

"Very true although, we didn't discuss that aspect." The

man said as he placed the bottle back on the table and stepped back.

Jack raised his glass. "To us?"

Erin responded in kind. "To us." She sipped the liquid and her eyes rolled back. It was pure ambrosia. She had tasted many wines in the past, but this was no doubt the best she ever had.

Jack rolled the liquid in his mouth for a second before swallowing. "Wonderful! Better than I expected."

"I am glad you approve Monsieur. I always enjoy serving a man of your tastes." The man inclined his head then left.

Erin tilted her head. "What was that all about?"

"Just what I said. Many of his clients try to appear as though they know all about wine to impress the people they are with. He is so used to it that he assumed I wanted the same."

"So . . . you don't want to impress me?"

Jack grinned and looked off to the side. "Well . . . not in that way."

Erin reached across the table and took his hand. "I know. And I will give you a chance to impress me later. Although, this is certainly off to a good start, anchovies aside."

"I am not going to live that down am I?"

Erin grinned. "Maybe some day."

"But not today?"

"Right." Erin cut off a small piece of chicken and ate it. The flavors mixed with that of the wine enhancing it further. "But then again, there might be a way . . . " Her eyes gleamed.

"Which is?"

"Later." She said with a grin that went from eat to ear.

When they finished, another man appeared pushing a cart loaded with cheeses. Looking at the large selection, they couldn't decide and asked the fromager. He nodded, selected several cheeses, cut small wedges of each, placed them on small plates in front of them. Erin snapped another photo. The man chuckled. "Enjoy," he said before departing.

Erin slipped a small piece into her mouth and savored. She sipped the last of her wine causing a mini explosion of tastes in her mouth. "I don't think I ever had cheese quite like that before."

"Nor I. It sure beats Velveeta doesn't it?"

"Oh gosh yes!"

Their main waiter appeared and after removing the used plates, he returned with dessert. Erin's eyes popped when he placed the Creme Brulee in front her. The small plate held a vanilla custard, caramelized with several small black marks, then adorned with a strawberry sorbet. Flicks of black pepper dotted the otherwise smooth sorbet. She snapped another picture as the waiter smiled. "Please enjoy." He then placed a small folder to Jack's right and left.

She slipped in a spoon and the rich taste of strawberries and vanilla cream exploded in her mouth. Her eyes went wide. "Wow."

Jack grinned. "And you didn't want dessert. I told you it would be worth it."

Erin slipped another spoon full into her mouth and swallowed. "Yeah yeah yeah. Aren't going to let it go are you?"

"Tell you what, I'll let you off of the hook if you let me off as well."

Erin smiled. "Deal. But I reserve the right to keep my plans I have for you tonight."

Jack threw back his head and laughed. "Oh I love you. Deal!" He opened the small folder, and without blinking put several large bills inside and closed it leaving the money sticking out of the top a quarter of an inch.

When finished, they placed their spoons in the center of the plates, napkins on the table, and stood up. Erin looped her arm through Jack's and they started to leave when their waiter returned pushing a different cart. "Monsieur, please do not forget your mignardises." He pointed to the jars on the cart that contained several different bite size treats.

"Ah, we almost did." Jack pointed to several chocolate covered items. "Those look good."

Erin nodded. "I will take one of those too. I could never resist chocolate."

Jack glared. "What are you talking about? You usually say it will nuke your diet."

She squeezed his arm and lowered her voice. "Shhh. And weren't you the one to say I should have dessert?"

"Well, technically this is after dessert, dessert," he whispered back.

"Oh hush. Yes one of those chocolate pieces please."

The waiter nodded. "Of course. Chocolate dipped candied orange zest, it is one of my favorites as well." He extracted them from the jar using a small tong, placed them on small separate plates, and handed them over.

Erin popped one in her mouth and she chewed slowly. The chocolate melted in her mouth while the orange zest would satisfy the ultimate sweet tooth. She swallowed. "Wow."

"They are impressive. I don't think I've had anything like that," Jack said.

"I am glad you approve." The waiter took the small folder, opened it then pointed while tilting his head. "Monsieur?"

Jack smiled as he put the small now-empty plate down. "No change."

His eyes went wide. "Thank you Monsieur!"

Erin gave Jack a questioning look as she put the small plate down on top of Jack's, but she waited until the waiter left. "What was that all about?"

"He was thankful for my tip. That's all." Erin looped her arm back through his as they left the private dining room.

"How much did you tip him?"

"Well them actually, as it will be spread around to the other waiters that served us."

"And how much?" she whispered.

"Enough to make them happy."

"Which is?"

Jack's grin widened. "Enough."

She squeezed his arm. "You aren't going to tell me are you?"

"Nope."

As they approached the front door, the man that greeted them smiled. "I trust you enjoyed your time at Le Bloch's?"

Erin nodded. "Yes very much thank you."

"And Monsieur?"

"Yes, and be sure to thank your staff for the excellent service," Jack said.

The man inclined his head. "I certainly will. I hope you come again. Enjoy your day."

Jack pulled a phone from his pocket. "Yes, we are done and standing in front of Le Bloch's." He put the phone back in his pocket.

Erin leaned on Jack's muscular shoulder. "Mmm I don't want this day to end."

"It hasn't yet."

Erin looked up. "What do you mean?" The limo pulled up and Jack opened the door for her before the driver could get out. He walked around to the other side, nodded to the driver and climbed in. They were heading down the road a few seconds later.

"We aren't going home?"

Jack's grin could have swallowed the sun. "Nope."

"Then where are we going Mr. Winecker?"

"Some place special."

Erin crossed her legs causing the nylon to rustle. She slapped him on the arm with a gleam in her eye. "Are you going to tell me?"

"Nope, it's a surprise."

Erin sighed as she gazed out the window. "You're no fun."

"On the contrary, I think this is a lot of fun." Jack grinned.

After about an hour, they pulled up in front of an iconic movie theater. Erin tilted her head. "A movie? You are taking me to see a movie? Why the big secret?"

"You'll see." Jack hopped out of the limo, went around, and helped Erin out. She noticed several people looking at them, the limo, then back again. Erin held his hand, and he leaned closer as they walked towards the entrance. "It seems we have a few fans." He pointed with his head.

"Probably wondering who we are."

Inside all the staff were wearing iconic theater uniforms. The women wore skirts with a red vest jacket over a white blouse. And the men had black pants, white shirt, and the same red vest. The men also had little hats. Jack paid for the tickets and an attendant showed them inside to their seats. The theater was not anything Erin had expected. The walls were covered in rich paneling with prism lights embedded in the recessed ceiling. Other lights reflected up towards the ceiling at various intervals along the walls. The seats were not your typical theater seating, but lush padded chairs that resembled high quality leather office chairs. As they sat down, the seats squeaked, further enforcing the thought they were leather.

In front, a giant golden curtain extended down over the screen. Above, a balcony extended out over them. She assumed it contained more seats. Erin glanced around again then leaned over to Jack. "I didn't know they even made theaters like this anymore."

Jack smiled as he turned his head. "They don't. I heard about this place, and it is scheduled to be taken down next month."

She leaned closer. "Why? This place is gorgeous."

"Yes it is, but it is also under used. Look around, not many people here. And this is a new movie. The building is also old and there was talk of it needing work, but the owner couldn't afford it."

Erin looked around again. "Work? I don't see anything that needs to be done. This place is amazing."

"I know. Sad it is a bit out of the way, and with fewer people going to theaters than they used to, it is the final nail in the coffin."

Erin nodded. "It is sad. I noticed the movie coming in. 'Mr. Right'? You bought me to a romantic film?"

"Yeah? I had no idea." Jack's eyes gleamed.

She swatted him. "You did too. But I expected something with more–"

"Action?"

"Yes."

"Well ..." Jack trailed off. "I think there might be some action in this one too."

"Ah-HA! I knew it!" She swatted him again. "I knew you

couldn't just bring me to a romantic movie. Not without being under duress."

He leaned close again. "I am not that bad."

"Oh yes you are. Well, except for this week, which has been wonderful."

"I told you I am trying to–"

"I know, I know, you are trying to make up for the past. But no one changes that fast."

Jack smiled. "Yes they do, if they realize what a wonderful woman they are married to and haven't been treating her right."

Erin melted into his arm. "You keep saying things like that and I am going to start believing you."

Jack kissed the top of her head. "There is no chance of that stopping, so you had better get used to it." He took her hand into his and squeezed.

"I don't think I ever will. So you will just have to keep trying."

He nibbled her ear that was just under his chin. "Oh I intend to."

The lights flashed several times indicating the movie was about to start. Erin removed her head from Jack's chest and sat back in her seat. The lights dimmed, Jack squeezed her hand again and smiled. "I think you are going to love this."

The movie was a wild ride of humor and action. They both laughed out loud several times and enjoyed the whole film. When the lights came back up Erin looked at him. "We seem to have the same luck with our dates lately."

Jack's eyebrow rose. "Are you saying that I am killing people when I pretend to go out to the parking lot?"

"Well no, but you have to admit that the last few dates have had something bad happen."

Jack winked. "But I told you third times the charm." His ear twitched and his eyes darted around. "Did you hear something?"

"No, I didn't. What did you–" A loud cracking sound ripped through their ears as a column near them split in half. Fishers appeared in the balcony floor directly above. They grew exponentially spreading throughout the area. When they met, the structure released its tension as dust, dirt, seats, flooring, carpet, and lights fell straight down. "Jack!" Erin screamed and grabbed for him as she closed her eyes.

The smell of acrid sulfur stung her nose. She gagged but didn't dare let go. A moment later when everything was quiet she opened an eye and looked around. Jack was smiling. "Erin! Are you okay?"

She opened the other eye. "Yes I think so. What was– " Turning her head, she saw while they were unharmed, all around them resembled a war zone. Large sections of seats were flattened under the weight of the balcony that was above them a few minutes ago. Only a nearly perfect circle surrounding both Jack and Erin was untouched. Even rebar that should have punched through Erin, was bent straight up instead. "What in the world? How are we still alive?"

Jack shook a bit as he shrugged his shoulders. "I don't know. Looks like we got lucky."

One of the attendants rushed over to them. "Are you two all right?"

Erin gave a somber nod. "We seem to be."

"Thank God. I have been telling them we should have closed last month, but the owner had given the closing date to the media, making it difficult to change."

"Why are you closing in the first place? This is a wonderful theater." Erin sighed. "Or rather was."

"We noticed a few stress cracks in the foundation. Nothing that age wouldn't account for.   And it didn't make the building unsound. Nor did we ever find an issue with the balcony. With the decline in attendance, the owner decided to close. But I had a bad feeling and urged him to close sooner. He told me a month wouldn't make any difference." She sighed looking around the giant mess of dirt, seats, wiring, rebar, and plaster. "Looks like I was right."

Erin didn't know what to say. She kept trying to make her mouth work, but words refused to come out. Jack stood up and took Erin's hand. "Come on, let's get out of this mess."

"Are you sure you're all right? I think we should get you checked out." The attendant said. She refused to cross what was left of the fallen balcony, preferring to stay out from under it in case gravity won and pulled down the rest.

Jack nodded. "I am sure." Erin stood up and nodded then started trying to walk through the mess. She stumbled twice. It proved difficult to navigate in normal shoes, let alone high heels. Without a word Jack reached down and with two strong arms swept her off of her feet. He carried her through the rubble without even flinching.

"I could have walked."

"I know, but if it messed up your shoes, I would have never heard the end of it." Jack smiled and managed to give her a slight squeeze.

Erin smiled back. "Of course, these are my only designer pair."

"Uh-huh, I thought so. Dodged that bullet."

By this time they had reached the lobby area. Erin kissed Jack on the cheek. "You can put me down now you know."

"Oh I don't know. I like sweeping you off your feet."

Erin thought about the last three days and wondered what

was really going on, but decided to play along. "You do all the time."

"Yeah, when our dates are not life and death incidents," Jack grumbled.

"Well it is not like you planned this." She watched his eyes. "Or did you?"

Jack stopped and put Erin down on the sidewalk outside. "Erin! How could you even *think* that?"

"You do have to admit is very strange."

"Heck yeah, but I certainly didn't want it to happen! Good grief, why would I keep doing it? If this keeps up, you will want to leave me as you might think your life is in danger."

The thought had crossed Erin's mind, but she pushed it away. "I am not going to leave you. I love you. But I do wonder what the heck is going on!"

"Erin, honestly, so do I!" Jack pulled out his phone. "Yeah, it's me. We are out front. Pick us up." He put the phone back into his jacket pocket. "The limo will be here in a minute. He had to park over a mile away because of the size."

Erin folded her arms and gazed off into the setting sun. A cool breeze whipped through causing her dress to ripple and sent a shiver up her spine. "Good. It got cold all of a sudden."

Jack took off his jacket and placed it on her shoulders. "Here this should help."

"Thanks," Erin mumbled.

A moment later the limo appeared and Jack helped Erin in then opened the door on the other side. "Take us home please." He hopped into the limo and shut the door. For most of the ride Erin sat in silence, looking out the window as her mind tried to make sense of the last few days. She felt his hand on hers and she turned to see his pleading eyes. "Talk to me."

"What about?"

"What about? You are a million miles from here and you ask me what about? Please say something, the silence is deafening."

She turned away. "What would you like me to say?"

"Anything. My tie isn't on straight, my shoes are scuffed. Something!"

She turned her head back. "Well, your tie isn't straight and your shoes are scuffed."

"Dang it Erin! You know what I mean! I didn't have anything to do with these accidents. They are accidents nothing more. We should be thankful to be alive, not arguing why we are."

"Who is arguing?"

"Erin! Please!"

She sighed and gazed into his eyes. They pulled at her soul and she remembered how Jack never could lie to her. His eye would always twitch when he did. And she could only remember one time when he tried to get away with it, and that was for their honeymoon. "All right, I believe you. But did you tell anyone else of the plans of our dates?"

Jack shook his head, sighed and leaned back. "No. Again, that is why I think they are freak accidents. I didn't tell anyone, so how could this all be arraigned? Sure Le Bloch's required a reservation, but nothing else did. I did call for the limo, but that wasn't ordered ahead either."

They pulled up next to their house and Erin hopped out before Jack could get around to the other side. "I'll meet you inside."

"Be with you in a minute, I have to settle up with the driver," Jack said getting out his wallet.

Erin walked upstairs and into their bedroom. She kicked

off her heels and sat on the bed. Her mind whirled over the events of the past few days. She stood up and unzipped her dress and hung it back up in her closet. Jack slipped two big arms around her waist, pulled her close and nibbled her ear. "Not tonight, I have a headache."

"Uh-huh," Jack mumbled. "And why don't I believe you?" He continued nibbling and moved down her neck.

Every part of her body responded to his electric touch. She knew his movements, everyone of them screamed Jack, but better. She couldn't explain it. But what about the accidents? Her head said no, but her heart beat with his. The void between her legs ached for him. "Oh the hell with it," she thought. "I will figure it out ... tomorrow." She spun around and kissed his lips igniting a fire that burned all night long.

$$-7-$$

A light on a console flashed several times before a long white finger pressed it. A voice chimed "System syncing with the council. Established and displaying." Above, the large screen displayed several hooded people seated around a semi-circular table.

One from the edge nodded. "Status?"

"Landing was without incident. Everything is progressing as planned. Monitoring and carrying out orders as instructed."

The figure third from the center leaned forward. "Are we certain that this is wise? Shouldn't one operative be plenty?"

The center figure rolled his eyes. "The time for discussion on this subject is long past. We have agreed this is the best course of action giving the nature of the mission. You know what will happen should a failure occur."

The third nodded. "Of course. But shouldn't we at least give them the chance to complete the mission before we send someone else?"

"In normal circumstances, I would agree with you. In this case I do not. We cannot afford to wait. And the rest of us agreed."

"I know. It seemed wise at the time, but now I wonder

about the wisdom of that decision."

"As I said, it is a little late for such thoughts."

The third one pointed at the screen. "No it isn't. He can return. Nothing more need be said."

The long white finger on the screen rose up. "Chairman, if I may."

The center figure nodded. "Of course."

"The mission may be best served if we continue as planned, both finish our assigned tasks, then submit our reports. The situation is dire enough that two confirmations would be advantageous."

The hooded figure on the far right grunted as his fingers tapped the table. "You assume that the findings will be the same."

The watching figure nodded. "Yes I do. But more importantly I believe in the mission. I would not be here otherwise. In the end my findings will outweigh his, and I am sure you agree."

The chairman nodded, his hood going back and forth as he did. "Yes of course. Your standing with the council has not changed, nor has the wisdom of what you say."

A grunt was heard from the end of the table.

"Unless someone cares to contest that?"

The figure on the end began to raise up, then thought better of it. "No, I do not contest the wisdom of what has been said."

The chairman sat back in his chair. "Then everything will proceed as planned."

The long finger twitched. "Thank you chairman, I shall get to work. I will communicate again when I have further information on the situation." The giant image in front of the table flickered then disappeared.

The chairman looked up and down the row of figures

seated behind the table, their hoods still pulled up as was tradition. "Unless there is something else, I suggest we consider this session completed."

The hood on the end turned towards him and grunted. "I would, but I do not see a point in it."

The chairman turned. "Please, if you have an issue, we wish to hear it."

The eyes hidden by the hood narrowed. "No you don't. My position has not changed, but it has been ignored."

The chairman stood up. "You have been heard several times, and out voted at each opportunity. If you wish to do so again, the council will hear you."

Another grunt was heard as the figure stood up. "I do not see the point in wasting further time with those lacking ears. The condition is fatal, we know that. We also know there must be a cure. To look outside is frivolous. We do not need anyone else. We can do it ourselves. I also think the public should be informed of the full situation."

The chairman balked. "And have a mass panic? Have you lost your mind? This has been raised before and we agree it is not the proper course of action. You alone hold this view."

The standing figure nodded. "Yes I do. But just because I stand-alone, does not mean I am wrong." He turned and walked towards the doors. When his hand reached the panel, the chairman called out.

"Do remember that you are bound, by the rulings of the council. You know the punishment for doing otherwise."

The hooded figure turned back towards the table, and the figures still sitting behind it. "I do. But I also think it almost might be worth it." He left, and the door closed before the chairman could say anything more.

Jane sat at the kitchen table tracing the wood grain as she sipped her coffee. "You make the best coffee. What's your secret?"

Erin pointed to the stainless steel carafe between them. "That is part of a pour-over brewing system."

"Is that all?" Jane sat back. "I thought there would be a lot more to it."

"Well, that and a lot of love."

"Ah-HA! So there is more to it you aren't telling me." Jane laughed and took another sip.

Erin chuckled. "Perhaps, but if I told you, why would you ever come here?"

Jane glared and sat down her mug. "You know I don't come here for your coffee."

"I know," Erin said with a smirk. "But you know I had to say it."

"I suppose. Now do you want to tell me the real reason why you invited me over?"

Erin blinked fast. "What ever do you mean?"

"Don't give me that look. I have known you too long to fall for it. The only reason you would call me over like this is you have a bee in your bonnet about something. Is that stud-muffin of a husband done something stupid again?" She caught Erin's darting-away eyes. "I am betting yes."

"Well ..."

"Come on girlfriend, spill it! Or do I have to resort to extortion?"

Erin chuckled. "No you don't." She stood up and walked over to the kitchen window.

"What is it? We're not getting any younger you know."

"I know." Erin turned around, leaned back against the sink and crossed one leg over the other. The denim made a slight rustling sound. "You're right, in that the problem is Jack. However, I don't know how to explain it."

"Give it a try. I am sure I can fill in the blanks."

Erin gazed out into the living room. "I am not so sure about that." She looked back to the woman seated at the kitchen table and sighed. "It is like this, we have been on dates for the past three days and–"

"What a minute! You mean that stud-muffin took you on THREE dates one after another? And you are complaining? Tell you what, if you aren't happy let's switch husbands."

Erin cleared her throat. "Would you let me finish?"

"Sorry. But I did tell you I would fill in the blanks," Jane said with a sly smile.

"Well wait until I finish before you do. Anyway, we were on three dates. And they were wonderful. But … each one … had … incidents."

"What do you mean 'incidents'?"

"The first day we almost drown, the second the roller coaster crashed, and the third a balcony fell on us."

Jane choked spitting what coffee was left into her cup. "Hold on. Are you telling me those accidents were you?"

Erin blinked. "What do you mean?"

"Girl haven't you been following the news? Those accidents were all over the news feeds. I thought it was separate couples, they never did have names or photos. Which I am surprised at, considering how fast news is these days."

"Yeah, that was us. Every time we left before anyone else showed up. I guess either no one saw them happen, or didn't have their phone. Jack hustled us out of there quick. Which I agreed with, I only wanted home after."

"I can imagine. You are having one bad week."

Erin sighed. "Yes. While the dates otherwise were fantastic, one accident is scary, two is odd, by the time three happens you have to ask yourself what the heck is going on."

"Yeah I get ya, but how were they otherwise?"

"As I said, wonderful. Almost dreamy, we did things we haven't done in years. It felt like it was back when we were dating. Then the nights, oh gosh, they were far–"

Jane raised her hands. "I don't want to hear your sexcapades with that stud-muffin. It will only make me drool, and then you would have to clean up the floor."

Erin grinned. "Sorry."

"No problem, wish I had it so good. Speaking of which, so you had three wonderful dates except for the accidents?"

"Yes."

"Anything else odd other than that?"

Erin shook her head. "Not really, except for the nights that were–"

"I told you I didn't want to hear it. You'd be drowning in drool. So what is the problem? They say bad things happen in threes. You had a freaky, bad week. Nothing more. Or is there something you aren't telling me?"

"No, other than my feeling something is different."

"Like what?"

"Well, I don't know. It is hard to explain. He is more attentive, loving, especially when we–"

"Will you stop with the drool fuel? Sheesh!" Jane lowered her head and shook it back and forth. "Her stud-muffin husband is going nuts over her, treating her like a queen and she is complaining."

Erin walked back over to the table and sat down. "When you say it like that, it does sound like I am being silly. But what about all the accidents?"

"You had a bad week. I've had three weird things happen in a row like that, but I admit not to that level. Still, odd things happen. Unless it keeps up, I wouldn't worry about it."

"I guess you are right," Erin said leaning back in the chair.

"Of course I am. So where is that stud-muffin husband of yours, anyway?"

"He went to work."

"I thought you said he had two week's off? Did they call him back that soon?"

"No, I forced him to go. He tried to plan something else for today and I–"

This time Jane couldn't contain herself when she choked and ended up spraying the last of her coffee all over the kitchen floor. "You WHAT!?"

"Sent him to work."

Jane got up, walked over to the paper towels, and started cleaning up the mess she made. "Girl, sometimes I don't think you have your head on straight."

"What do you mean?"

Jane shook her head then sighed. "You are hopeless, completely hopeless."

"I am not!"

"You are! How many women have dreamed of being with their husband the way you are right now, and when he tries to take you out again, you send him to work? Give me a break!"

Erin slouched in the kitchen chair. "I blew it, huh?"

"Oh, let me think a sec ..." She raised a finger to her chin and peered off into the distance for a half a second then looked back at Erin. "Heck yeah!"

"I will call him in a minute and see if he still wants to spend the day together."

Jane sat back down, her arms folded across her chest. "I am willing to bet that answer will be yes."

"Jack, you didn't need to come in today. I told you I could handle everything for the couple of weeks." Ethan said as Jack inspected the new sawblade and its supports.

"I know, but I wanted to double-check a few things."

"Uh-huh, Erin made you come in today didn't she?"

Jack stopped and turned to face Ethan. "H ... h ... how did you know?"

Ethan folded his arms and gave a lopsided grin. "It is written all of your face."

"It is?"

"You look like a man that offered up the best proposal ever, only to be rejected. Since I know you didn't do that, want to tell me about it?"

"Not really."

"But you will?"

Jack laughed. "Sounds like I don't have a choice."

Ethan shook his head. "Not unless you want me to tell the rest of the guys, and they will be hounding you night and day."

"That's extortion."

"You bet. And what kind of partner would I be if I didn't try to help? After all, you grumped at three guys in thirty minutes. They are going to gang up on me if I don't do something."

"That bad, huh?"

"Yep, so what did Erin do this time?"

"She didn't want to go on a date today."

Ethan frowned and cocked his head. "She didn't want to go out with you? Where were you taking her? A truck rally again?"

Jack laughed. "No, I learned my lesson from the last time. I was planning on taking her to the aquarium and have a nice dinner afterwards."

"Okay, so what did you do? For her to turn you down, and you to act like this, you must have done something."

"It wasn't me, our last three dates didn't go exactly as planned. Something always came up to kill the moment." Jack thought about telling Ethan the details, but decided against it.

"That's all? There must be more to it than that."

Jack shrugged as he checked the torque on the last bolt. "Not really."

"Well then go home and take out your wife! Make this date memorable."

Jack groaned. "The last three were memorable enough."

Ethan didn't blink. "Then make sure this one goes well. It isn't rocket science you know."

"So says the single guy," Jack grinned.

Ethan rolled his eyes. "I just haven't found the right one, unlike you. But I do know how to treat a lady. And you have one heck of a woman there. I have been trying to tell you that for years. Glad you finally took my advice to heart."

"All right, I will call her right after this. Okay?"

Ethan clapped Jack on the shoulder. "Good and let me know how much the dinner is. My treat."

Jack's eyebrow went up. "You sure?"

"Why do you think I pushed you out for these two weeks? You both need time together. Believe it or not, I do hear things."

Jack smiled. "I know you do."

"Besides, it will help with moral around here. The guys might organize a sit-in until your mood improves. And we will never get the upgrades done."

Jack laughed as they stepped back several yards and waved to the man at the controls. "Start it up. The new blade is ready."

The man in the control booth nodded. He checked the new computer controls, the monitor showed everything was ready. He activated the command and the giant sawblade started spinning, faster and faster.

"There! That should do it," Jack shouted. "This new blade, housing, and carriage system should double our output."

"I know," Ethan shouted back, "I bought them!"

There was an eerie squeal, then a mighty crack as the huge blade began to wobble. Jack faced the sawyer in the booth and waved his arms. "Cut it!" But before the power could be cut, the blade broke free of its mounting sending a wheel of death hurtling towards them.

Ethan's eyes widened then snapped shut as he braced for the impact. But it never came. The smell of sulfur stung his nose as he heard a loud bang. He opened his eyes to see the blade on the floor bowed and flattened on the one side. He looked closer, then turned to Jack who was still standing next to him. "What happened?"

Jack shrugged. "I don't know. Sounds like the mounting failed. Defect I suspect. I hope you still have the receipt."

The sawyer ran out of the booth and down to the two men on the floor. "Are you two all right?" he said wide-eyed.

Ethan ignored the sawyer. "That I know, I am talking about that!" He pointed to the flattened bit of metal that used to be a perfectly flat, round, almost a man tall sawblade. "What happened to it? It should be flat, not bowed on one side."

"Must have caught on the housing when it flew out."

"But shouldn't it have went in a different direction?"

Jack shrugged again. "I don't know. I'm just glad we are both alive to talk about it. And you do have that receipt, right?"

Ethan rolled his eyes. "Of course I do! But–"

"But nothing, we spent a mint on these upgrades and now a quarter of it is scrap metal." Jack pointed to the damaged blade and mounting system.

The sawyer studied both men and spoke a little quieter than last time. "Are you two all right?"

Ethan's eyes flared. "We're fine! Now tell me what the heck happened here?"

The man blinked. "Sir?"

"Did you see what happened?"

The man's eyes fell to the ground. "Not exactly."

"What the heck does that mean?"

"Well . . . I saw Jack, er Mr. Winecker waving and telling me to cut the blade's power. Which I was about to do anyway. I glanced down at my controls and reached for the button when I heard the crack then a split second later the bang. When I looked up, I saw you two standing with the blade laying on the floor in front of you. That's all."

"What about the camera system that comes part of the new conveyor?"

"It isn't hooked up yet," the man whispered.

"What? Why not?!"

The sawyer pointed to Jack. "Jack said we should get the blade and other systems functioning first."

Jack cleared this throat. "Sorry Ethan, I thought it was wise to make sure the conveyer, housing and blade worked before bothering with non-essentials."

Ethan blinked. "Non-essentials?! How can you say a camera that would have told us exactly what happened a non-essential?"

"At the time I thought it was, now I don't. I am sorry, okay?"

Ethan sighed. "I have to admit I probably would have done the same thing. We have operated the mill for years without one after all."

Jack nodded. "Right, that was my thinking as well. Call the manufacturer and have them ship the new parts. We should have them tomorrow if they express them." Jack walked over to the flattened blade and pointed. "Which I am pretty sure they will, given the circumstances." A dun da dun dun DUNNNN emanated from Jack's pocket and he pulled out his phone. "It's Erin. Sheesh how did she know so fast?" He tapped a button and put the phone to his ear. "Hi Sweetheart, what's up?" Jack nodded several times. "Nope, everything is fine here. Sure sounds good, I'll be home in twenty minutes." He put the phone back into his pocket.

Ethan pointed to the phone. "I take it she didn't know?"

Jack shook his head. "Nope, she said it was wrong to shoo me out this morning and wanted us to do the date if I wasn't busy and still interested. I assumed you wouldn't mind if I take off?"

Ethan's stormy face softened, and he smiled. "No, you aren't supposed to be here anyway. I will take care of this mess. Get out of here and give her a kiss for me."

The drive home was uneventful and when he opened the kitchen door, he found Erin in a deep red mini-dress that set off her green eyes perfectly, black nylon clad legs, and high heels. Jack's heart raced at the sight.

"Hello there Mr. Winecker, about time you got home."

Jack gulped. "Umm ...I wasn't planning on a fancy place today."

"That's okay, I thought I would pick instead."

His eyebrow rose as he closed the door. "Oh? So where are we going?"

"Our living room."

Jack blinked as he leaned forward and his head turned. "Our living room? But you are–"

"All decked out. I trust you approve?" She spun around to give him the full effect.

Jack felt certain areas of his body grow stiff before he could regain his control. "Yes of course. You look wonderful. But all of that for our living room? What are we doing?"

"A movie."

Jack blinked again. "A movie? You look hot enough to stop a train in its tracks, and we are only going to watch a movie?"

Erin walked over to him with an extra sway in her step and letting her heels click extra loud. She wrapped her arms around his neck and pulled him close, then kissed him with all she had. When they came up for air she smiled. "I know you like this dress, I can tell." She leaned in closer rubbing his manhood straining against the layers of fabric against her hip.

"And I just got it to go to back down before that kiss," Jack grunted.

Erin pulled him down and whispered in his ear. "Think of me as a beautifully wrapped present that you alone get to unwrap. That is something we can only do at home. So what do you say Mr. Winecker? Want to watch a movie with me?"

Jack grinned. "I would rather watch you."

"You still can, think of it as the appetizer. Dessert is later."

Jack's heart hammered against his chest. "Gosh don't know if I am going to live past the appetizer at this rate."

She nibbled his ear and then went down his neck. "Oh I am sure you will survive. I will make sure of it. After all, I have plans for you." She leaned back, grabbed his shirt and led him into the darkened living room.

— 8 —

Erin awoke feeling like she went 100 rounds with the heavyweight champion of the world.   While she fully intended to wear Jack out, the man's stamina was unbelievable.   After several orgasms, she was reduced to a loveable pile of goo, and Jack was still going strong. In the end, she collapsed into a deep sleep while Jack was still nibbling her ear and whispering how much he loved her. At least they had moved upstairs to the bedroom before that happened.

She reached for Jack but and found him gone …again. Climbing out of bed she peeked between the blinds and saw Jack's truck still in the driveway. Erin listened carefully but not a sound emanated from the house.   She sighed and hopped into the shower hoping it would revive her pleasantly complaining body. After the shower, looking in the mirror she saw the glow and grin from last night. "I had better avoid Jane today, or she will never let me hear the end of it."

After getting dressed, with still no sign of Jack, she called his phone. The dun da dun dun DUNNNN ring tone came from downstairs. "Well that answers that," she muttered and went down to the kitchen to make breakfast.

Jack was walking fast through the forest when a man appeared in the distance. "K'lan! Why haven't you reported?"

Jack squinted. "Who are you?"

"I am shocked! Do you not recognize your old mentor?" The man said coming closer. He was older, with a few wisps of white hair, deep lines on his face that screamed age, but the rest of his body said something else. His jacket failed to hide the muscles bulging underneath. If it wasn't for the face and hair, one would think he was younger than Jack.

"Ra'Toth?"

"None other."

Jack took the last few steps closing the distance between them. "What are you doing here?"

"I would think that was obvious."

"I haven't sent my reports."

"Correct. You know the mission cannot move forward without them."

"I am well aware of that. I have been very busy gathering the data and verifying."

Ra'Toth leaned back a bit as his eyes narrowed. "Then everything is on track? Or have there been unforeseen circumstances?"

Jack shook his head. "Everything is progressing properly, and the mission is on track. I will send the reports soon."

Ra'Toth folded his arms. "And you are sure the verifying has only slowed the delay of the reports, not the mission timetable?"

"I would have told you if there were. There was no need for you to come all this way."

"Oh *au contraire*, I think there is. You know how important the mission is, our survival depends on it."

"I don't know if it would go that far, if we fail here. There is still time to try again elsewhere."

"The council does not agree with that assessment, that is why I am here. And why I have completed the report."

Jack gulped. "You have?"

"Yes, and it is as we suspected. We can use the people here to cure us of the genetic illness. I shall send the report when I have completed a few final conformation tests."

Jack thought about a physical conflict with Ra'Toth, but he knew his mentor was far stronger than he appeared. "I see, and what do you need of me?"

"For one thing, I would like you to do the job you came here for."

"But you said–"

"Never mind what I said, I still want you to complete the task. While the council will ignore it, it will still show you did your job. And while we are on the subject why are you spending so much time with this human female rather than your mission?"

Jack blinked then his mouth hung open for a moment before he realized and closed it. "You have been watching me?"

"But of course. I am your mentor, what would you expect?"

Jack's eyes narrowed. "The council told me to blend in. That is what I am doing."

Ra'Toth's eyes went wide. "Blend in? So that is what you call indulging in time with this female?"

"Yes, of course. You disagree?"

Ra'Toth studied at his hand, made a fist, then folded his arms. He glared at Jack. "I would not say all the time is justified. Especially since you have many other options open to you."

Jack stiffened. "I acknowledge that I have other options, but this one is best. I have run many simulations as to the outcome. And I have been here longer than you. Do you not agree that I could have more first hand experience thus far?"

"While unlikely, I do not have the information to counter your argument at this time. Therefore, I will let you continue as you see fit. But be forewarned, if I see a reason to change this assessment, you must submit. There will be dire consequences otherwise. Do I make myself clear?"

"Yes. Perfectly clear Ra'Toth."

"Good, then this meeting is concluded. I shall return before I transmit the report, or if I see a reason to intervene in your performance."

"Of course Ra'Toth." Jack bowed, and he smelled sulfur. When he straightened, there was no sign of Ra'Toth. Only the wind blowing through the trees of an otherwise empty forest.

Jack continued walking in the same direction and checking every few steps to make sure he was not being followed. In the middle of an empty area devoid of trees he placed his palm shoulder-high into the air. At first nothing happened, then a beam of light ran up and down his palm. A hole in the universe irised open in front of Jack and he stepped into a bright hexagonal corridor. The door sealed itself after.

"Kan? Status?"

The wall adjacent to him shifted as made of clay as a screen appeared in the middle then extended a couple of inches from the wall. It flashed and flickered as Kan spoke. "Hello K'lan. I did not expect you for several units. Status is as follows: All systems nominal. Nothing to report."

"Are you sure? There has not been anyone trying to access you or the ship?"

"Sir, I am certain of it. If there was, I would have stated in the status update."

"Sorry. But I had to confirm."

The screen continued to flash. "While I am not capable of emotion, the apology is appreciated nonetheless."

Jack smiled remembering that Kan was not a person, but his semi-intelligent Kryllin Automated Network. While he had expanded Kan far beyond the standard, it still lacked emotions. "You may not have been located, but how about Ra'Toth? Have you seen him?"

The screen brightened more than any other time and didn't dim. If Jack didn't know otherwise, he would swear Kan was showing emotions. "Ra'Toth? On this planet? No, the last time I made contact was the spin before our departure. Why do you ask such an odd question?"

"Because I saw and had a conversation with him less than thirty points ago."

The screen brightened further. "That is very unusual. If Ra'Toth is indeed on this planet, he did not follow protocol and contact us before landing. Therefore, his mission is one of secrecy, even to us. Which considering we are the first to land on this planet, and are the only ones for the council to approve of doing so, makes the situation even more problematic. It also begs the question, how long has he been here?"

"You took the words right out of my mouth."

"A interesting choice of human words, and I am sure quite correct."

"We have some work to do. Meet me in the control room."

The screen flickered. "Sir, you do realize that I am all over the ship?"

Jack laughed. "I do. But it is something one human would say to another."

"But I am not human."

"Let me rephrase, something one colleague would say to another."

"That I can accept." The screen went dark and disappeared into the wall.

Jack walked down the maze of corridors to the central top that contained the bridge or command center. A chair reformed into his human proportions as he approached it. "Can you access the central network without being seen?" He sat in the chair as it moved forward and several screens folded around him.

The nearest screen flickered as others scrolled with data. "Negative. At this distance the narrow beam would be located within thirteen points."

"But not before that?"

"Possible, but not likely. And Sir, if I may ask, why are we continuing to use the less efficient human communication?"

"Because I am under cover at the moment, prefer it in this form, but more importantly Ra'Toth will not expect it."

"The last reason I can understand."

"Good. Now do you think we can access and download the council records in ten points?"

"It depends on what data you require, and how narrow your search. You will also need to link or I cannot access such records."

"I can do that, but we will need to be faster. Less than ten points, or Ra'Toth might detect it being the only other Kryllin on the planet."

"It might be possible, depending on the data you require."

"I want all records of the mission, the genetic illness, and any references that connect with Ra'Toth."

The screen went dim then brightened several times as if it choked. "Sir! You do realize that the data on the genetic illness that plagues your people covers thousands of years? It will take much longer than the time allotted to download."

Jack grinned. "I think I may have an idea how to do it." Jack placed his palm on the screen as his eyes closed. His hand deformed into a red and black shimmering blob that spread up his arm. A moment later his hand and arm resumed their previous shape.

"Very interesting idea, Sir. If I use this code to command the entire Kryllin network to do a super compressed flash feed of all the data, it should not take longer than the time required."

"But will it work?"

The screen flickered several times. "The code is sound, but I have no way to prove it without actual testing. To my knowledge, this has never been done before."

"No one had a reason to before. Will it be detected?"

"Because we are using the entire unused network for such a short period, doubtful. However, if someone is monitoring very closely at the time, then yes."

"I guess it is a chance we have to take." Jack sat back in the chair which leaned back. "How long until you are ready for the attempt?"

The screen flashed. "I am ready now."

Jack sat up. "Let's get this over with." He placed his palm on the screen and it again changed shape into a red and black shimmering mass.

The screen flashed. "Accessing the network. Using your credentials. Problem, access restricted."

Jack redirected his mental energy and could see the

restrictions. He also saw the signature, sealed on Ra'Toth's order. His mentor assumed he would try this. But Jack knew a trick that even his old mentor may not. "Kan if we can't go through, it's time to go under."

"Sir?"

"Never mind, let me direct."

"Acknowledged."

Jack concentrated, and they went down, down, down, into the ancient network's maintenance sub-systems. Systems built so long ago, and worked so well, that many forgot they were there.

"Sir, seven points remaining until detection."

Sweat poured down Jack's human face as he tunneled and pushed into one of the oldest of the systems. And he found what he wanted: a back door. A emergency connection built by the system architects so many millennia ago. Jack pushed his way in and they emerged inside the council's sealed records. "Kan you know what to do. You should have full access from here."

"I do. Running code." The entire network momentarily blinked.

"Whoa, I saw that."

"Let's hope no one else did." Numbers, data, images flooded onto Kan's adjacent screens. "Flash feed is operational." The screens continued to change faster and faster.

Jack's body shook several times, and he fought to steady himself in the chair. "Do we have enough time?"

"Unable to estimate. I could expand the feed further, but we would be detected. As humans would say, I don't dare do anymore."

"Hurry," Jack said his voice weak.

"I am, Sir. Three points left."

"Ugh."

"Fifty micro-points left …forty …download complete severing the connection."

Jack fell back into the chair as his hand reformed. "Did …were we detected?"

"No. The download completed with twenty micro-points to spare. And thanks to the enhanced access, I was able to delete any record of us being there or the download itself. The only sign would have been at the start of the feed when the network blinked. In all probability, most Kryllin would assume a momentary glitch, and ignore it."

Jack sighed. "Most people are not all."

The Kan's screen brightened. "That is correct. However, there will not be any record or any other proof of our access. Without that, I cannot see anyone suspecting."

Jack relaxed as the chair reformed into a straight lounger. "Bring up the information that the council has on Ra'Toth's mission."

"That was sent near the end of the data stream. It will take some time for me to decompress and reorganize for such access."

Jack yawned. "Sure, let me know when you do." A moment later he was fast asleep.

"K'lan? K'lan? I am finished, please wake up." Jack didn't move. "Hmm, this should work." Kan raised and lowered the chair so fast that it hit the back of Jack's head with a soft thump.

"Okay, okay, I'm awake. You didn't need to do that." Jack said rubbing the back of his head.

"I beg to differ Sir. You were in a deep state due to the

exertion during the link." The screen brightened. "Now, what are we looking for?"

Jack sat up. "Display all the information with regard to Ra'Toth and his mission here."

"Displaying, although there isn't much."

Jack read over the screen in front of him. "Hmm, you are right. Nothing specific other than being sent here. That is not good."

Kan's screen blinked several times. "Why, Sir?"

"Because if the council-who is notorious for its record keeping- didn't log the reason for him coming here, then they were afraid someone might find out. And I have to assume that someone is me."

"Your logic is sound."

"Display all the information about the illness, flash feed."

"You realize that even at that speed, it will take many time units for you to finish? The link would be faster."

"I know, but I am still weary and wouldn't retain it anyway. Commence flash feed."

"Acknowledged."

Data flashed on the screen in front of him at a blurring pace. Jack took it all in as best he could. He needed to figure out what the council was up to, and it must be hidden in the data. Since he didn't know exactly what he was looking for, Kan couldn't help. It was up to him.

Jack's face went ashen. He found an obscure reference to a deeply hidden report. "I think I found it."

Kan piped up. "Which is?"

"There is a report buried in several layers of estimates on what would cure the genetic problem we all suffer, it cites the cure might be found in the human population. But the required genetic material would necessitate the use of more than half of the population." Jack sat back. "I don't know why I have never seen this before. I was told I had all data on the disease."

"I may be able to answer that. Due to the unorthodox access method, I was able to get far more data than your normal clearance level."

Jack's eyes went wide as his head went back into the chair. "My people don't plan to coexist. They plan to conquer."

Jack dug through the data for several more hours but couldn't find anything that disagreed that his people did indeed plan to conquer the Earth. "I must stop this but how? Our people have time to find another solution. I could try talking with Ra'Toth, but if I do that he will know I am against the plan. And more importantly, I know more than I should."

The screen next to him flashed. "I agree. The situation is difficult. I have no solution to propose."

"Unless I stop Ra'Toth."

"How, sir?"

"By any means necessary."

$$— 9 —$$

It was well past noon and Erin started to become worried. She called around, but no one knew where Jack was. Not even Ethan, Frank, or any of his buddies.

She glared at the reluctant phone in her hand, sighed and dialed Jane. The phone picked up after several rings. "Hello?" She sounded tired.

"Jane! Have you seen Jack?" She heard the rustling of large cotton sheets.

"No, why? Is that stud-muffin missing in action again?"

Jane sighed. "Yes, I can't find him anywhere." There was a long pause on the other end of the phone. "What's wrong?"

"Nothing, I was taking a nap. Up all night with a design that is driving me nuts. Did you call his friends?"

"Yes, even Frank. His buddies haven't seen or heard from him today."

"Well, knowing the last few days you've had, I still think he is planning something for you."

"Without his phone?"

There was another rustle of cloth as Jane sat up. "He left his phone?"

"Yes! Although, he did a few days ago too."

"And he never did before?"

"Nope."

"Hmm perhaps he thinks you could track what he was doing by tracking the phone. It probably has GPS doesn't it?"

"Yes, but I never would–"

"Doesn't matter. He might think you would and wants whatever he is doing to be a surprise."

"I don't–"

"Listen, you need to get your mind off of this. Tell you what, I will be by in five and we will hit the mall."

"Go shopping? I can't do that, what if Jack calls?"

"You are taking your phone right?"

"Yes, of course, but–"

"But nothing! If he needs you, he will call. Leave him a note and don't worry about it."

Erin rocked back and forth then sighed. "I don't know."

"Listen this my treat, so you had better get your butt outside when I get there or I am coming in after you. Got it?"

Erin laughed. "Okay girlfriend see you in a few."

Jane pulled up a little while later and Erin hopped in. Jane's eyes went up and down. Erin was wearing her skinny jeans, wedge sandals, a semi-tight t-shirt, and her makeup had more of a night-time flare. "Is something going on I should know about?"

Erin blinked. "What do you mean?"

"Girl, you look like you are going for more than a fun *me* day at the mall."

"Well this is what I normally wear when Jack and I go."

Jane's one eye narrowed. "And I am guessing that look is what you used to get him out of the house and shopping?"

"Yes. Although, we haven't went in a while."

Jane snorted as she shifted into drive and they took off down the road. "Based on the past few days, I doubt you would need to. That guy doesn't know what he has."

"Actually, he has told me he does. Several times in fact."

Jane glanced over. "The past few days I am guessing?"

Erin shrugged. "So?"

Jane shook her head. "He wakes up, realizes what a wonderful woman he has, and you doubt his every move. People can change you know."

"Not like this they don't."

"What are you saying? You think he is not Jack? Come on! You told me he walks like Jack, talks like Jack, and knows everything that Jack knew. How could he be an imposter?"

"I know I shouldn't have complained. But I am trying to take your thoughts to heart and putting it out of my mind for now."

"Uh-huh. You sure look like you are."

"Hey! I told you, this *is* how I look when Jack and I go shopping. It is not like I am looking for another guy or make Jack jealous. If I wanted that, I would have worn a short dress with pumps."

"Uh-huh."

Erin rolled her eyes. "So where are we going?"

"I saw this new restaurant opened up and thought we could get a late lunch, do a bargain hunt, then catch a movie. Sound like a plan?"

"It will be after dinner time before I get home!"

"So? You didn't have plans."

"But what if Jack calls?"

"I told you, if he calls I will have you home faster than you can say 'Jack Rabbit'. Deal?"

Erin laughed. "Deal girlfriend, deal."

A short while later they pulled up to the mall and Jane found a smaller parking place near the front. She slipped into it and smiled. "Sometimes I love this car."

Erin slung her purse over her shoulder as she got out. "I never understood why you got this. It seems like a good breeze would blow it over."

"Not at all! It is heavier than you think. And it still gets great gas mileage. But you know the best thing?" Jane asked as they walked inside.

"No, what?"

"That lump of a husband I have wouldn't be caught dead in it!"

Erin laughed. "He never drove it?"

Jane shook her head. "Nope. Making that little thing is all mine. It's the perfect husband repellant, and I didn't even have to paint it pink."

Inside the air was cooler, and they hit one of the bargain stores first. While the prices were low, so was the quality and nothing caught their eye. After several stores, they came across the new restaurant Jane had spoke of. A bright red sign with backlit letters proudly said "Moteki's" They went inside and a waitress approached them wearing authentic traditional Japanese dress.

"Irasshaimase," she said bowing. "How many in your party?"

"Two please," Jane said.

The lady bowed again. "Follow me." They followed the woman who could only take tiny steps in her tight, silken, dress. It was shorter than a traditional dress, coming up to the knee, but the style was otherwise authentic right down to the golden cherry blossom design. When they reached a table in the corner she gestured and they both sat. She placed two

English menus in front of them and smiled. "I will return in a few minutes."

Erin watched her wiggle away. "You would think they would allow her to have a dress with a bit more room."

Jane gazed over her menu without looking up. "I suspect the owner is male, after all would a woman name her place Moteki's?"

Erin chuckled. "You're probably right."

"Darn right I am."

The waitress returned and placed a wet towel near each of them. "Are you ready to order?"

Jane sat down her menu. "Yes I think I will have the Katsudon."

The waitress nodded. "Katsudon, anything else?"

"Nope breaded pork with egg over rice is plenty for me."

"And what would you like?" The waitress said looking at Erin.

"A salad thanks."

"And?"

"Nothing else."

Jane rolled her eyes. "Girl, I told you it is my treat, you can order more than that."

"I ate something before we left."

Jane's eyes narrowed. "You lie."

Erin shifted in her seat. "All right, and the Tofu Teriyaki."

The waitress wrote something more on her pad. "Tofu Teriyaki and plain salad, I will return when it is ready." She left and Erin watched her pass the order, then greet two more customers that entered.

"Girl, you need to stop worrying so much about your figure."

"And you are going to lose yours eating like that."

"Why bother? The lump I am married to wouldn't notice if I gained five hundred pounds. He doesn't touch me, regardless. I still wonder if he is gay."

Erin giggled. "You have a point. But still no reason to let yourself go."

Jane blinked. "Who said I am? Don't you know Japanese portions are small? It's not like I ordered a t-bone steak, vegetables, baked potato smothered in butter, with apple pie for dessert."

Erin raised her hands. "Okay, okay you win. Now what is the towel for?"

Jane picked up one and proceeded to wipe her hands. "It is for cleaning your hands. I thought you liked Japanese food?"

"I do, but we always did take out, not eat in."

"Well not all of them offer wet towels. This one seems to be more authentic than most."

A few moment later the waitress returned with their orders, placed them on the table and left. Erin opened the chopstick packet and held them up. "I am not sure I can do this."

Jane raised up a piece of pork with a practiced hand. "It is easy. Hold the bottom one along the base of your thumb and resting on the ring finger and the top one with your thumb and index finger letting your middle finger be the fulcrum." Jane held up her hand. "Like this."

Erin tried and after several attempts she held a piece of tofu up with her chopsticks. She grinned and slid the slippery food into her mouth. A moment later she swallowed and smiled again. "Is very good."

"See I told you would get the hang of it. This place might be new, but once a few friends mentioned it, I knew I would have to come here."

Erin ate another piece of tofu and swallowed. "I'm glad you talked me into it."

Jane smiled. "About time you admitted it."

Erin choked. "Good thing I wasn't drinking my tea at that moment, or you would have had a bath. I'm not that bad."

"It still would have been worth it. And no you aren't. But I had to say it anyway." Jane said slipping another piece in her mouth.

They chatted about which store to hit next and they decided to visit several of the clothing stores next. Jane made eye contact with the waitress who came right over with their bill, and she paid at the cashier near the entrance. They walked across the polished tile to the opposite side where one of the nicer clothing stores were located. While the quality was good, nothing caught their eyes, and they continued on.

After three more stores, Erin suggested a designer dress shop and Jane's eyes went wide. "There? I am surprised. They are so expensive."

Erin nodded. "True, but looking is free."

"Can't argue with that," Jane said with a shrug.

Inside the smell of new clothes increased even though the selection was less. They pored over the various displays but didn't see anything much of interest. Jane walked back outside and turned towards Erin to find her gone. She turned around and saw her looking at a dark blue dress on a mannequin. It was short with a plunging neckline held up by spaghetti straps, form fitting bodice with lacing in the back, and the whole dress shimmered when the light hit it in certain ways. Jane walked back inside and saw the stars in Erin's eyes. "I think you found something."

Erin didn't turn. "Hmm?"

"I said, I think you found something."

Erin shook her head as if to break a spell. "Oh no I didn't. Let's go." She started to walk out when Jane planted a hand on her chest.

"Where do you think you're going?"

"I thought it was obvious, out of this store."

"Uh-huh, before even trying it on?"

Erin blinked. "Try what on?"

"Try on what on she says," Jane snorted. "How about that dress you were drooling over."

"I wasn't drooling."

"Maybe there isn't any drool on the floor, but you had stars in your eyes that were so big that they had to be super novas."

"They weren't that bad."

"I beg to differ. So go try it on."

"Why?"

"Because as you said looking is free."

Erin's eyes moved quickly between the walls and floors. "Why do I suddenly feel trapped?"

Jane grinned. "Maybe because you are? So go try it on."

Erin grumbled and asked the clerk to remove dress from the mannequin. A few moments later she disappeared behind one of the red curtains that covered several small rooms in back. When she emerged Jane's draw dropped as her eyes traced the contours of Erin's body framed beautifully inside the dress.

"Wow. If that don't light the fires of your stud-muffin husband, I don't know what will."

"You think?"

"Do I think? You have got to be kidding. It might even work on that lump of a husband I have. I would try it, except I would fall out of the top."

Erin giggled. "Yes, you are much more endowed than me."

Jane folded her arms. "That's putting it mildly. Ah well, it wouldn't have worked anyway. I don't think I could light a fire under him unless I threw him into a bonfire." She paused looking up and down the dress again. "So, are you going to get it, or just stand there all day and look at it?"

"Nope. Looking is free, buying is not," she said heading back to the small rooms.

"Look, I told you it was my treat today right? Well get the dress, I will pay."

Erin peeked out around the curtain. "Are you nuts? No way am I going to let you do that."

"You talk like you have a choice."

"You wouldn't."

"Oh I would. I haven't seen a dress light up those eyes like that in a long time. So yeah, you are getting it. And if it happens to help your relationship with Jack, all the better."

"You're doing this to prove a point aren't you?"

Jane looked up towards the ceiling and raised her hands. "Yes! She can be taught!"

Erin finished changing and slipped through the curtain. "Hey!"

"Just kidding." Jane smiled then her look hardened. "But you are not getting out of here without that dress." She pointed to the garment in Erin's hand.

"All right, you win."

Jane smiled. "Don't I always?"

"Not always, but often, yes."

The clerk wrapped the dress, placed it in a designer box, then handed it over to Erin. But before she could say anything more, Jane whipped out her credit card and handed it over. Erin was about to say something, then thought better of it. The clerk looked at Erin with a bag and pointed to the box.

"Do you want it in a bag, or do you want to hold it like a long lost relative?" Erin's cheeks went a light shade of red when she realized how she was holding the box and handed it over. The lady placed it in a large fabric bag with reinforced handles. "There you are. Since you are a new customer, the bag is included free. Have a good day."

Erin leaned closer to Jane as they left. "Are you sure about this?"

"Will you stop! I can treat my friend once in a while."

"But it was–"

"Expensive, yes I know. But my designs are doing well. And you forget that husband of mine does bring home a good paycheck, even if he is a lump. But I will make you a deal."

"Yes?"

"I want the details of what goes on when you wear that dress for Jack."

Erin laughed. "You got it."

They hit several other stores, but didn't find anything of interest. By that time the movie was almost ready to start. They made a mad rush to the theater and made it just before the lights dimmed. The film was forgettable, but good enough for a few laughs. When they got out it, the sun had set.

Erin checked her phone as they got into the car. "Still nothing from Jack. Not even a text."

"You sound surprised?"

"Well, I am. I figured he would have called me by now."

"Didn't you tell me, he doesn't have his phone?"

"Yes, but why still not call me?"

"Perhaps he can't at the moment. I think you worry too much."

Erin's eyes went wide. "But all day?"

"I am sure it is nothing."

"But–"

"Look, my lump of a husband shows up later than this many nights and never calls me beforehand. I never know when he will be home. There have been more than one dinner he had to reheat because he came home so late. He never complained, but never tried to call me ahead of time either. I suspect that Jack is busy with whatever he is doing and forgot."

"But when he is not even supposed to be at work today?"

"Didn't you think he could be out with friends?"

"Yes, but as I told you, I called them."

Jane's eyes narrowed as she shifted the car. "All of them?"

"Well . . . er . . . not all. I don't think I know them all."

"There you go. All this worry for nothing. If he doesn't come home tonight, then worry. But I think he will be home by the time we get there, or close to it. Why not call home and make sure since you are so worried?"

Erin shook her head. "No, I will wait until I get home. You are probably right and he is home waiting for me."

"I am. You will see."

After another good twenty minutes Jane pulled in and let Erin out. She walked around to the other side and Jane rolled down the window. "Thanks for the time out girlfriend."

Jane rested her arm on the retracted window's rubber gasket. "Anytime. You call and I will be there."

Erin leaned over and placed her hand on Jane's. "Thank you. It means more than you could know."

Jane smiled. "Oh I know. Now go have a good time with that stud-muffin husband for me. And I want *details*. M'kay?"

Erin laughed as she straightened up. "I told you I would."

Jane chuckled. "Well here's hoping." She headed off rolling up the window as she drove.

Erin sighed and turned around and took several steps placing her hand on the doorknob.

$$-10-$$

Erin walked into the dark house and flipped on the light. "Jack? Are you here?" No response. "Blast him! He is still gone. Where the heck did he go?" she muttered. She walked upstairs and checked the other rooms, still no sign of him. She sighed and walked towards their bedroom. She found the door closed and smelled sulfur again as she reached for the doorknob.

It turned, and the door creaked open but didn't see anyone. "Strange," she thought, "I know I didn't leave the door closed." Erin stepped inside, laid the cloth bag on her dresser, and looked around. Nothing seemed out of place. Her nose wrinkled at the sulfur smell, then her eye met a strange floor lamp in front of the window. It matched the rest of the decor, but yet stuck out like a sore thumb. "Where did this come from?" She reached for it then her eyes flashed in realization. It seemed fantastical, but yet made perfect sense. She was right all along. "All right whoever you are. I have had about enough of this. You think I don't read science fiction? Who are you and what did you do with my husband?" Erin again reached for the lamp but started to melt. The smell of sulfur grew stronger. In mere seconds it had liquified covering a small area on the floor.

Erin stood there as the primordial ooze grew in size. It started as a small shimmering puddle, then quickly magnified into the shape of a naked man. Her husband's face smiled. "How long have you known?"

A shiver ran through her but she stood fast as her nose wrinkled again at the smell of rotten eggs. "Since we made love."

"But how? I replicated your husband's methods perfectly. I downloaded his mind. I know every thought he ever had."

"Yes and that is why."

"I am sorry, I do not understand." Jack said taking a step closer.

Erin took a step back. "It was too prefect. No man could send a woman to sexual bliss that way every time. No human man anyway."

He sighed. "Well I did my best, I am sorry it was not good enough."

She shook her head. "Oh you misunderstand, it was wonderful, I have no complaints."

He blinked. "Then why–"

"Because once I realized you were not Jack, I had to find out who you were. And now I do, but one question remains."

He folded his arms and peered into her deep green eyes. "Only one?"

"Well the most important one to me. Where is my husband!?"

The form in front of her sighed. Walked over to a window as Jack would do, gazed out at the grass below, took a deep breath, and turned around. "I am sorry to tell you he is no longer functioning."

"You killed him!"

"No, I did not. But he saw me land and the exhaust gasses from my ship proved toxic to him. He should not have been there, I should have been invisible. But I admit, I did not check before landing. I had become lax after hopping all over the planet and assumed such a remote area at night was uninhabited. When I realized what happened, I did what I could, but it was not in time to save him. I never intended to harm anyone. I scanned his mind and saw the affection he had for you. I did not wish you to be without him so I took his place. I was sent to observe, and this would as you say, kill two birds with one stone. Fulfill my mission and make you happy at the same time, it is what your husband wanted."

"And what is your mission?" She said through narrow eyes.

"To prepare this planet for our arrival."

"Your arrival?"

Jack sighed again. "You see, we are slowly dying. Long ago we were not much different from you. But then began the age of genetic alteration. Little changes at first, then we became more bold. A project was created to eliminate all disease and aging from our bodies. And after hundreds of years we did find it. It also gave us our shape changing abilities. However, it was only until much later that we found out the terrible price we had to pay."

Erin tilted her head. "Which is?"

"We doomed our race in the long run. While we are almost immortal, our ability to procreate has been diminishing. It has now been centuries since any births have taken place."

"Oh that is awful."

Jack walked over and sat down on the bed. "Yes. I was sent

to try and see if a cure is possible using your genetic makeup as a template."

Erin blinked and sat down beside him. "My genetic makeup?"

"Well not yours per se, but humanity in general."

"Then why come here?"

"Well two fold, one it will require a vast amount of research time and the diversity of the whole human race. Therefore, we need your help."

"And the second?"

Jack sighed. "Our projections indicate that our sun will go nova in approximately two thousand years. While that might seem like a long time to you, it is not for us. However, we will have to move at some point anyway. But if you don't want us here for the long-term, we will find somewhere else to go. And as I said, we have time on our side." Jack walked over to the dresser, placed both palms on it, leaned forward, hung his head and sighed. "At least this is all what I was told."

Erin blinked. "Excuse me?"

Jack straightened and spun around. "The truth is another aspect entirely."

Erin cocked her head looking at the naked man backlit by the window, not sure what to make of this. "What do you mean?"

"What I have told you is the truth, but today Ra'Toth showed up."

Erin shifted her position on the bed. "Ra'Toth? Who is that?"

"My mentor. Because he did not communicate with me before landing, his mission is secretive, no matter what he says. Based on this, I tried to find out why he is here. I managed to break into restricted council files. While I couldn't find anything with regards to his mission, I did find something far more disturbing. They don't plan on coexisting, but conquering."

"Are you sure? Could it have been an error in the records?"

"Yes I am sure it is not an error. I have spent the entire day going over the files. While they were careful not to leave a trail, I know I have found the truth."

"Then what are we going to do?"

"Well I–what do you mean we?"

"I mean you and I."

Jack folded his arms. "Now wait just a minute, I'm not going to involve you. I have done enough damage in your life."

Erin stood up, pulled Jack over to the bed, and sat him down. "You may not be the real Jack, but you have shown me more real affection in the past few days than he ever did. I know it, don't try to deny it."

"But I–"

"Don't give me that. Now that I know what is really going on, how in the world do you think I could sit on the side lines while this all plays out? This is *my* planet after all, not yours. I think I have the right to help you defend it if I want to."

Jack smiled. "I get the feeling that I am not going to win this battle?"

Erin fluttered her eyes and sat him back on the bed. "Why Mr. Winecker, whatever do you mean?" She sat down in his naked lap, stroking something under her before he could object.

"Erin! Cut that out!"

"Ah, I wanted to make sure it still works." She said with an evil grin.

Jack's face became more flustered. "I told you I duplicated

his body perfectly, so what he would feel …so do I! Cut it out!"

Erin wiggled her hips. "Do we have an agreement then?"

"Yes! Please stop, we have work to do."

Erin grinned. "Good. But still, I am sure a quickie won't hurt."

"Erin!" Jack thought of throwing Erin off, but afraid of hurting her, he refrained. By the time he had formulated a plan how to extract himself from the situation, she had slid down her jeans, panties, and sat square in his lap. "I told you we don't …" he felt himself slide inside her "have time …for …for …"

Erin batted her eyelashes and wiggled some more taking his full-length inside her as their hearts began to race. "Uhh ohhhh don't have time for what?" She wiggled even more.

"Oh the heck with it," Jack said. He moved with her faster and faster. Erin removed the pants and panties the rest of the way, turned, and wrapped her legs around Jack. Their hips met and parted over and over again. Sweat beaded on Erin's forehead, but she didn't slow, only moved faster. Then she felt volcano inside her bubbling, ready to erupt. Her muscles clamped down tightly on Jack as she screamed and he shot into her again and again.

She fell around his neck kissing him. "Now see? Always time for a quickie with your wife."

Jack smiled. "Technically, I am not your husband."

Erin shook her head and kissed him again. "Nope. You are better than he ever was, in so many ways. But since you took his place," she pointed to the ring on his hand, "and wear my ring. Wouldn't you say that makes us married?"

Jack looked down at his hand then back into her green eyes. "I suppose so."

"Good, because you are stuck with me."

Jack smiled. "To be honest, I couldn't have asked for anyone better to be stuck with. There is no one like you among the Kryllin."

She leaned forward and kissed him again. "Good, now that is out of the way, do you have a plan to stop Ra'Toth?"

"I think so. It is risky, but I don't know what else I can do."

"Then do tell."

"Not yet, I have to make sure it will work before I tell you."

Erin sat up. "Are you kidding?"

"Nope. Can you blame me for wanting to make sure before we go any further? As I said, it is very risky."

Erin's eyes went to the hard wood floor then back up. "I suppose not."

"You wait here in the house, I will be back in a unit."

Erin eyebrow rose. "A unit? What's a unit?"

"Oh sorry, one of your hours. Sit tight, I will be right back." Jack stood up and walked out of the bedroom.

A minute later her eyes went wide, and she ran after Jack. She smelled sulfur again when she caught up with him and he was wearing clothes. "I was going to ask, 'Don't you need clothes?'." She pointed to the check shirt and blue jeans he now wore. "When did you put them on?"

"After I left our bedroom."

"But how? All your clothes are in there."

Jack grinned. "The same way I look human."

"So those clothes are a part of you?" Jack nodded. "That is how you got dressed so fast the other times?"

Jack nodded again. "It's not that I didn't ever wear any actual clothes. But sometimes I formed my own instead. There are several advantages."

"I can imagine, needing to clean them being one."

Jack laughed. "Yes I suppose that is one, although I never thought of it before. But I do have to create the clothes after I have taken human form. It is too difficult to build them with the human body and get everything else right. Well, at least for me anyway. Also, the less complex the object, the easier it is. Which is how you caught me as the lamp. I was testing a different form and by the time I detected you, I didn't have time to assume my normal shape."

"But you were wearing the ring without clothes." She pointed to the golden circle on his left hand.

"Oh, Jack, the real Jack never took it off. As a result I have that as part of his body. It is different from clothes and is always there."

Erin nodded. "I always wondered if he ever took it off."

Jack shook his head. "He never did, nor will I." He bent forward and kissed her cheek. "I will be right back."

Jack made his way through the forest being careful to take an unusual path, he couldn't risk being followed. He reached the devoid of trees and after one final check, he held out his hand. A hole irised open in reality as before, and he stepped through.

A screen emerged from an otherwise smooth white wall. "Greetings K'lan, I did not expect you for some time yet. Is there a problem?"

"Nothing more than before, and I need to figure out a way to stop Ra'Toth," Jack said as he walked towards the central area.

The screen disappeared into the wall, then reappeared near Jack. "I have devoted all of my spare processing to the problem, and have failed, as of yet, to come up with a solution." The screen disappeared again and reappeared in the central control area as Jack entered.

"I am sure you have. It has also been on my mind as well. But as the humans say, I am drawing a blank."

"Drawing a blank, Sir?"

Jack entered the command area and sat in the chair which conformed around him. "Meaning, I have no idea."

"Sir, I am detecting a life form near the ship."

Jack sat up. "I suspect it is one of the planet's indigenous life forms, a lot of them live in or near forested areas."

Kan's screen flashed. "No, this one resembles the form you currently wear."

"Ra'Toth? He has found us?"

"Negative. This is a female, human female to be precise. From what I know of Ra'Toth, he would never take such a form."

Jack nodded. "You are correct, he does not have any appreciation for females. Kryllin, or otherwise."

"Sir, the female is feeling the outside of the ship. Shall I activate emergency procedures?"

"Yes, but show me who it is first." The large screen flashed on in front of him filling with Erin's smiling face.

"Jack? I know you are in there! Let me in!"

"Activating emmergen–"

"Stop! Cancel that." Jack leaned back in his chair and sighed. "Open the portal and let her in."

"Sir? Are you serious?"

"Yes that is Erin, my wife. Let her in."

"Sir? You are married now? A lot must have happened in the time units since you were–"

Jack sat up and his eyes narrowed. "Just open the dang door!"

The screen went dark then flashed again. "Acknowledged. Portal open. She is entering. Portal closing behind her. Would you like me to instruct her to our location?"

"Negative, I will go talk to her myself." Jack stood up and left the control room.

Erin followed Jack, which is not to say it was easy. Quite to the contrary. He back tracked so many times in different directions that she lost him twice. But when she saw him place his hand out in midair, watched as a hole opened in the universe, and he stepped through, she knew it was the right place. She walked up slowly and felt around. After a few minutes her hand stopped but there was nothing for it to touch. Yet something was there. She moved her hand back and forth several times. "Jack! I know you are in there. Come on out! Or let me in, either way you are not getting rid of me this easily." A hole to her right opened up and she could see a white corridor. She stepped through and turned around in time to see the door seal itself. "Looks like I really stepped in it this time," she muttered.

Jack tapped her on the shoulder. "Yes and no. I thought I told you to stay home?"

Erin spun around. "Don't do that! It is bad enough I am in an alien space ship without you sneaking up behind me and going boo."

"I didn't say 'boo'."

Erin grabbed her chest. "No, but you might as well have." She glanced around the white corridor. "Nice ship you have here."

Jack folded his arms. "Oh really? And how many space ships have you seen?"

Erin smiled. "This is my first one."

"Then how do you have any comparison?"

"I don't, but it still looks nice."

A screen extended itself from the wall. "K'lan, do you want me to remove her?"

"Kan, if I wanted her removed, I wouldn't have let her in the first place. Until instructed otherwise she is to be given every courtesy. Is that clear?"

"Yes Sir." The panel disappeared back into the wall.

Erin placed her hand on the solid wall that was liquid a

moment ago. It felt smooth and cool to her touch. "Yes quite the ship you have here. K'lan? Is that your name?"

"Yes, but I would prefer you call me Jack."

"Works for me," Erin said with a shrug. "I like it better anyway. Who is Kan? A member of your crew?"

Jack gestured towards the hallway and took her hand. "Something like that." They walked corridors and up to the central control room and another chair formed and Jack pointed to it. "Have a seat."

Erin noticed the various screens scrolling with data, but didn't see anyone else. "So where is Kan?"

A screen emerged from the wall and flickered as it spoke. "I am Kan. Short for Kryllin Automated Network."

Erin raised an eyebrow. "You're a computer?"

"I find that remark insulting. I am far more than a mere computer, I am a network of–"

"Kan, later."

"Yes Sir." The screen disappeared back into the wall.

"He shouldn't have emotions, but I think I have expanded his systems to the point he does. At least on some level, and that proved it. Now, what are you doing here? I told you to stay home."

Erin folded her arms across her chest. "And I told you, you are stuck with me. I am not going to let you do this by yourself. This is my planet remember?"

"I know that, and I was coming back. I only needed to consult with Kan."

Erin sat down and turned back and forth in her chair. "Uh-huh. Then why did you take so many detours to get here? Hmm?"

"To make sure I wasn't being followed. But it would appear I failed."

"Never underestimate a wife that is tracking her husband."

"What? You humans can track–"

"Relax, I was joking. You did lose me, twice. I only managed to find your ship because I know the area. Jack, the old Jack, used to come here to star watch. I figured it might be big enough for your ship, and you mentioned he died where you landed. Soooo–"

"Elementary my dear Watson?"

Erin nodded. "Exactly."

"Well it makes me feel a little better that my methods were not at fault."

Erin pointed at the displays. "What is Kan working on?"

A screen emerged from the wall and flashed towards Erin. "I am attempting to find a way to stop Ra'Toth."

"Any luck?"

"As of this moment, no."

Erin turned towards Jack. "Wait a minute, you told me you had a plan."

"Er, well I do."

"Which is?"

Jack shifted from one foot to the other. "To get rid of Ra'Toth."

"Nothing more than that?"

Jack sighed. "At the moment, no."

"Well you certainly sound like a typical human male. Say you have a plan, when you don't have a clue," Erin sighed. "How about knocking him out?"

Jack shook his head. "Our physiological makeup is very different from yours. It won't work. And even if I could, he would send the report when he woke."

"Report? What report?"

Jack sighed. "I neglected to mention that. You see, I was sent here to examine humans and see if they could help us with our problem."

"I know that."

"What you don't know is I was supposed to send my data every spin, sorry, day, with my progress. I decided to do more research and verify everything rather than send possible error laden reports every day. Still, preliminary analysis wouldn't have taken me long. And I assumed the council would not care if I was a little late since time is on our side."

"But you were wrong?"

Jack nodded then plopped into his own chair. "Yes, Ra'Toth was sent in secret to find out why I had not sent anything. He has done his own tests and found the same thing I did. Your genetic make up might work as a template to cure us. But it will take time to know for sure."

"So what's the problem?"

"Ra'Toth is going to send his report if I don't. At that point there will be no way to stop the Kryllin from coming here."

"Can't you talk with him? It sounds like you have known him for a long time."

Jack shook his head. "No. While we have known each other for longer than humanity has been civilized, he is certain in his conclusions. In his eyes this is the only way to save the Kryllin, nothing else matters."

"Could you falsify the data? Say it won't work, while still doing your research in secret?"

"While I could do that, Ra'Toth will know. More importantly, so will the council."

"But it would be your word against his."

"Yes, and while he is not a full member of the council, he is darn close. Close enough that they would not believe me at all. And even if they didn't believe Ra'Toth, they would send someone else to investigate, who would confirm the same findings."

Erin ran a finger across her lips back and forth as she thought. "How long before Ra'Toth acts?"

"Tomorrow, maybe the day after before sends his report. I told him earlier today I would send mine. He will at least wait until tomorrow to make sure I haven't sent it. He also said he would visit before he sent his, but I can't be sure."

"I still think there must be a way to knock him out."

Jack shook his head. "No Erin you don't understand. That won't work."

"Why not? You are the same species, you should be able to take him on, knock him out, or whatever."

"I told you it won't work. You see, we age differently than you. While you get weaker after you reach a certain age, we only grow stronger. He is thousands of years older than I am, and hence far stronger than I."

"Even with the genetic problem you mentioned before?"

Jack nodded. "Yes even with the problem." He sighed and looked around, then continued. "It doesn't kill us, only weakens the ability to procreate. It is rather embarrassing to say that our own experiments into longevity seems to have had an adverse effect on our ability to continue our species. While it gave us an almost unlimited lifespan, it also destroying our ability to increase our numbers. As I said, we have been searching for a cure for a long time."

"I see. Can't we tell him that humans would want to help?"

Jack shook his head. "While your physiological makeup is unique and similar to our own before the modifications. And it is possible the solution is locked in your genetic code. With careful testing, yes we could figure it out together. However,

Ra'Toth feels that the Kryllin do not have the luxury of time. Something I disagree with."

"I am sure many people would want to help, if you asked. I don't see why that won't sway his position."

"No it won't. The problem is he sees your people as cattle to be used and discarded rather than equals to work with. He will bring my people here, conquer your world, do experiments, and discard you after. Then likely stay here since our own world's sun is dying. Our sun has a few thousand of your years left, that is all. While we have found empty worlds we could colonize, I doubt the council will bother once my people are here."

"Is there someway you could fight him and win?"

"No, I told you he is far stronger than I."

Erin grinned. "Not even if you cheated?"

Jack's eyebrow rose. "Cheated? How?"

"You have this ship, can you use it to even the odds? Can you use it to hold him somewhere? I don't suppose this has a brig or jail?"

Jack laughed. "No it doesn't." Then a grin started in the corner of his mouth and spread to the other side. "You might be on to something. If I tell him of my experiments, he will want to see the data in my ship."

Erin cocked her head to one side as her eyes narrowed. "How does that help?"

"I can lead him into the central data chamber, then erect an energy field to keep him there. But it won't hold him for long."

"Then you can knock him out?"

"No, but I could destroy the ship."

Erin sighed. "Why do I think I am not going to like this plan?"

"Because you won't. And I will need your help with the energy field."

Erin leaned back in the big chair and blinked. "Me? Why me?"

"Because I will have to be with him if this to work. And I can't activate such a field from inside the chamber."

"Wait, why can't Kan do it?"

"Because of the safety protocols that are deeply embedded in his systems. I don't have time to remove them all."

"And why do you need to be inside?"

"Because he will think something is up if I don't go with him."

"I get that, but why blow up the ship?"

Jack sighed. "You have never seen an angry elder Kryllin before. That field won't hold him for long. He will break out, then contact the rest to come here."

"But what about you? You will be trapped with him."

"Yes, but I am hoping to be able to buy time and keep him there until the ship implodes."

"No! Please! There must be another way?"

"The only other way is after I escort him into the core, I find a way to step back outside for a micro point while you activate the field. But it is dangerous. He might escape, then all of your world will die. I can't take that chance."

"I can! And I will. You need me to help you right?"

Jack didn't like where this was going, he only nodded.

"Well then Mr. Winecker, if you want my help, that is the plan we are going to do."

"Then you might as well go home for now."

"Why?"

"Because Kan and I have work to do. Right now you can't

access the ship's systems with your mind, we need to build a bridge so you can."

The screen flashed. "Affirmative. At this moment your brainwaves are very incompatible."

"And no sense in you waiting around here. You can't help until then. I will get you when the modifications are done."

Erin folded her arms. "You will come and get me right?"

Jack smiled. "I told you I would, and I will."

"All right. See you soon," Erin said leaving the room.

"Kan will show you to the door."

Another screen emerged from the wall near Erin and indicated a direction. "This way please."

Erin awoke to a tender kiss. She leaned into it and her eyes cracked open like a couple of rusty hinges. She blinked. It was still dark outside and her vision resolved revealing Jack's smiling face. "Told you I would come."

She stretched as she sat up from the couch. "What time is it?"

"About four thirty in the morning."

Erin yawned again. "Have you been working all night?"

"Yes, but I think Kan and I have made progress. Will you join me?" Jack held out his arm.

"Like you had to ask." Erin stood up, looped her arm into his, and walked out the door. A short while later, they found themselves back inside Jack's ship. "Hello Kan." Erin frowned when he didn't respond. "What is up with him?"

"He is busy with another project." He pointed to a silver ring that sat on the work surface of the control room. The back of it had organic components that moved of their own accord and led down to a connection under the console allowing constant contact with Kan and other ship systems. "We spent all night building it. Put it on."

"Where?"

Jack smiled. "On your head. It is a head ring, or control ring if you prefer."

Erin picked it up. "Are you sure this is not going to fry my brain or something?"

"Erin, I would never tell you to put on a device if I was not certain–"

Erin held up her hand. "I was kidding." She sat the hard metal ring on the top of her head. While it fit, to say it was comfortable was a stretch.

"Try to access the core. Just like I told you, focus on the system and send the command."

Erin focused, but nothing happened. "I am trying."

"I know you are. These systems weren't designed for your brainwaves, you can do it."

Erin tried again and the door behind them closed.

"I did it!"

Jack grinned. "You did. Now once more." The door slid open, and closed again several times. "Good, I think we are ready."

"Ready?" Erin blurted. "You have got to be kidding me. I just opened a door a few times, I need more practice than that!"

"I wish we had the time, but if we don't get Ra'Toth now, he might contact my people. Which he could do anytime now."

"I thought you said he had to do several experiments?"

Jack shook his head. "I suspect that was for my benefit, giving me a chance to submit my own report before he did."

"He hopes you will do the right thing in his eyes?"

Jack nodded. "He may not put the welfare of this planet high on the list, but he does care for me."

"And you for him, I can tell."

Jack sighed. "Yes I hate to do this, but I don't see how we have any other choice. I will not have the blood of billions on my hands, I would rather see our race die out."

Erin placed her hand on Jack's shoulder and squeezed. "I know."

"I will go find Ra'Toth and bring him here. Make sure you stay inside this control room. I have set up some shielding in here. He shouldn't be able to detect you, but if you leave the room, all bets are off."

Erin nodded. "I understand." She stood up as much as the head ring and its connections would allow and kissed him. "Please be careful."

"Oh I will. Besides, you are not getting rid of me that easily." Before she could answer, he disappeared behind a bulkhead.

Erin sat back in the self-conforming chair. "Kan, do you know any good music?" No response. "Kan? You there?" Still no response. "Wow, he must be really busy with something."

Jack wandered around the forest several times where he saw Ra'Toth before, but no signs today. He double-checked the area, liquified into a shimmering red pool, and reached out with his mind. There was something in the distance but he couldn't be sure. He reformed and headed off in a new direction. He was about to give up when he smelled sulfur and turned around to see Ra'Toth's smiling face.

"Hello K'lan. I was wondering if you would seek me out, or if this planet had taken the best part of you."

"You knew?"

Ra'Toth folded his arms. "But of course. Do you think I would have trouble detecting your feeble attempts to find me? To a Kryllin of my age, it was like a beacon in the middle of a storm."

"Then why did it–"

"Take me so long? It didn't, but I wanted to see how long before you gave up. A lot less than I had hoped. I thought I taught you better. Now I assume you have something you wish to discuss?"

Jack nodded. "Yes, would you come back to my ship? I have data I wish to confirm. Something unusual."

Ra'Toth's eyebrow rose. "Something unusual? Could you be more specific?"

"It would be best if I show you, but I suspect this latest data shows that the humans are not the cure we hoped for."

"All my findings indicate otherwise, I highly doubt you found to the contrary."

"Which is why I do not wish to send a final report to the council if my data is flawed."

Ra'Toth nodded. "I agree, it would result in your immediate recall and barred from any further missions for a considerable period of time."

Jack gestured in the direction of the ship. "Please Ra'Toth, I do not wish to lose my standing with the council." He turned and started walking.

"Very well, but why do you insist on using this primitive human movement? We could be there in a few micro-points otherwise."

"As you have said, I do not have your experience and

abilities. This way I know what is ahead and no one can happen upon us before we get there."

"Again, I do not find a flaw in your logic. There may *yet* be hope for you."

Jack dropped his head. "I am honored to hear you say that Ra'Toth." He led Ra'Toth to the ship in a roundabout fashion and after an hour they arrived. Jack held out his hand, and a beam scanned his palm. A hole appeared showing the white corridor beyond.

Ra'Toth's eyebrow went up. "You programmed the ship to acknowledge this human form? Why?"

"Again, I do not have your experience, I felt the extra caution maintaining the shape in case I was seen was warranted."

"Then you may take this experience from an elder Kryllin to heart: it is not necessary."

Jack lowered his head again as he stepped through. "Thank you Ra'Toth, as always I appreciate your insight." Ra'Toth stepped inside and the portal sealed behind him. Jack pointed to a lower section on the same deck. "This way."

Ra'Toth stopped. "Aren't we going to your command center?"

Jack shook his head. "No, I wanted to show you the source of the data in the core."

Ra'Toth tilted his head for a moment then nodded. "Very well, lead on."

They went through several thick bulkheads and entered the core. Screens flashed on several walls as diagnostics and other data scrolled past. They walked to the center and Jack brought a particular data block on the screen. "This is what I wanted to show you."

Ra'Toth leaned closer. "Hmm interesting, it will take me a

moment to decode this." His eyes narrowed as he reached out and placed a hand on the other panel.

"Of course." Jack took a step back. The jumble of characters on the main screen began to change into a readable form as Ra'Toth's mind accessed the decryption system. "Erin, if you are going to do it, now is the time," Jack thought.

Erin concentrated on sealing the core. "I must do this!" Her eyebrows met as sweat ran down her forehead. Nothing happened. She tried again. A subsonic *gling* was heard throughout the ship.

Jack's form liquified and lunged like water from a fire hose under high pressure. His opponent missed blocking by a microsecond and attempted to follow. A shimmer shot down from the ceiling of the core and intensified as one Ra'Toth's large tendrils bashed into it.

Ra'Toth impacted against the energy field with increasing force. "This cannot not hold me!"

Jack had reformed into his human shape and started running for the door then turned. "Maybe not, but it will for the moment."

"K'lan you will regret this! I should have stopped you rather than tested. But I gave you the benefit of the doubt. A failure I will not repeat twice!"

Jack stopped and turned. "What do you mean test?"

"Many of us assumed that you had defected and sided against us even though that would doom our race. Others in the council said you were loyal. I was one of them. But when I came and found you involved with that human, I had to find out how far. Our protocols forbid you from revealing yourself to anyone until our actual arrival. Yet time and time again you did. Risked exposure to save that female. Or someone like her. When I saw that, I knew we could no longer trust you with the mission: send us the data and prepare the humans for usage."

"You were behind all the accidents?"

Ra'Toth laughed that was a combination of shriek and gong that shook the room. "Did you really think so many incidents would happen by mere chance? I thought you better at computations than that."

"I knew they were not all by chance, but I assumed it was someone from this planet's government trying to determine my true identity."

Ra'Toth shimmered, and he felt the repulse of the energy field as he hit it again. "You have doomed our race!"

"No, if we don't find the cure here, we can look elsewhere. We have time. It isn't killing us."

"But it is! You don't know everything."

"But I do. I accessed the full database."

Ra'Toth laughed. "You don't have clearance for that."

"But I did. And I know you were the one that sealed it!"

Ra'Toth's tendril went a deeper red than Jack had ever seen as it bashed against the field. "You still don't know because we never put it in the central database! Can you imagine the panic among our people if the truth got out?"

"You mean–"

"Yes you fool, we are doomed! We do not have the time you think. Perhaps 100 cycles, if that. The oldest have already started to succumb. We do not have time to find another solution. The humans are all we have."

A red globe lowered from the top of the core and began flashing. A voice echoed throughout the ship. "Warning main propulsion system has been compromised. Implosion immanent. Evacuate immediately!"

Ra'Toth bashed on the field harder. "No!"

Jack smiled as the ship confirmed Erin had managed to drop the shield surrounding the main drive. "Goodbye Ra'Toth."

"You have not won! Even if I die, our people will come to this planet. You have changed nothing!"

"We will see about that." Jack hit the door lock on his way out and the massive crystalline facet closed sealing the outer data core. It wouldn't hold Ra'Toth but a few more seconds. But those few seconds might be needed should he manage to get past the field.

The ship began to shake faster and faster as the entire crystalline structure vibrated. "Warning! Implosion immanent!" Jack morphed into a large rounded wheel shape and rolled faster than his human form could run. He was almost near the exit portal when he felt Erin still inside the ship. He turned and dove back towards the control room with incredible speed. But she had already left and was heading towards him. "Erin! What are you doing? It told you to leave after the destruct was activated."

Erin stared at the massive red and black flashing wheel in front of her. "Not without you I'm not!"

The ship's vibrations reached a crescendo with an ear splitting screech. "No time! Hang on!" Jack reached forth with a tendril, grabbed Erin and pulled her to his middle holding her with several more tendrils as he began to roll faster and faster.

Erin put a hand to her mouth as the world spun. "Jack! I am going to be sick!"

"Sorry, can't be helped." The ship shook again as part of

a wall cracked and fell over towards the center of the ship. Then another. Pieces of the ceiling fell at an angle, again towards the center of the ship.

Inside the core Ra'Toth continued bashing against the field with increasing speed to the point all that could be seen was a red and gold blur. Then he backed up, reformed into a large spear head with a laser sharp point and ran it into the field at full force. It shattered upon the impact, unable to compensate for so much force in a tiny area. Ra'Toth leaped towards the door and hit it again in the same way. The crystalline structure split along the lines of the atoms then fell away. He was free! But as he tried to leave the core, he felt himself dragged back. "No!"

"Jack what is going on? I am feeling really heavy."

"Yeah, tell me about it. Did you eat a bunch of doughnuts or something?"

Erin put her hand back to her mouth trying hard not to vomit. "That is not funny. What's going on?"

"The ship is imploding. The gravity well inside the main drive has been released, and the ship is being sucked into it." Jack spun faster and reached forth with a tendril that reached inside a wall and pulled. He did it again and reached out for the exit portal as large pieces of corridor and equipment passed him falling into the black abyss at the center of the ship.

Gravity increased again and Jack began slipping backwards. "Jack!!" Erin screamed.

"Erin, I have an idea. Hold your breath."

"What?"

"No time! Do it!"

"Okay!" Erin sucked in a deep breath and Jack completely formed around her. She felt herself going back hit something then rocket forward at tremendous speed. Jack let himself fall back to a remaining bulkhead then using it as a launching point, centered all the energy he could into one massive thrust forward. They shot like a spring out of the ship and rolled down the hill a good thirty yards.

Jack pulled away from Erin who gasped as she sucked in several deep breaths. She leaned over and splashed hot liquid on the grass. "Don't ever do that again!"

Jack reformed into his human shape and held her hand. "It was the only way to save us." They glanced up in time to see the whole ship fall in upon itself in a blinding flash. All that remained was a slight indentation in the dirt.

"I don't get it. Isn't a gravity well a black hole? Shouldn't that have destroyed the whole world too?"

"In your understanding of them, yes. However, if you can control them, as we have learned, it is possible to have them seal themselves after a certain amount of material enters the void. Essentially, all the material of the ship falling into it caused it to cancel itself out. At least the artificial ones we make. The natural occurring gravity wells, are a whole another story."

Erin rubbed her temples. "If you say so. I assume with Ra'Toth gone, the Earth is safe?"

Jack shook his head. "Not exactly."

"What do you mean, 'Not exactly'?"

"I am sure he filed the report on his ship and set it to transmit in the next spin or so. He always had a backup plan. Now we need to find his ship."

Erin glared at him. "And how are we going to do that? Your ship is gone!"

"Oh ye of little faith."

Erin rolled her eyes. "Oh I have faith, that we are in

trouble. Did you forget that your ship had the ability to turn invisible?"

Jack laughed. "No, of course not."

"Then how are we going to find Ra'Toth's?"

"You'll see." Jack said grabbing her hand as they walked back towards the house.

When they reached it, Erin glared at him. "Jack, how are we going to find Ra'Toth's ship? Are you going to take our TV and build a ship tracker or something?"

Jack smiled as he tapped his chin. "Hmm, you know that might work."

She gave him a shove. "Will you cut it out!"

Jack laughed. "Follow me." Erin followed him into the kitchen and down past the cellar door.

She looked around but didn't see anything unusual. The bicycles, work bench, and a couple broken appliances they hadn't got around to throwing out were there as before. "There is nothing here."

Jack smiled. "Yes there is." He walked over and pushed on a brick. The brick slid in and a wall opened up revealing a hidden chamber with a large amount of equipment. There were displays, crystalline components, and a large box on the other side she had no idea what it was.

Erin walked around studying everything in the room. "You took this from your ship?"

Jack nodded. "Yes. I knew it would come in handy. Especially the fabricator."

"Fabricator?"

"Yes, it can create almost anything given enough time."

Erin's eyebrows rose. "Anything?"

"Well, it can't create a complete living being, but anything else. Yes. And this here." Jack said sitting down at a table and one of the displays that appeared to have a ship image flashing on it. "Is the central core. Or at least a backup of it. It isn't near as powerful as the original, but it does contain all the data."

The screen flashed. "It also contains me," Kan said. "Showing everything off, and what does K'lan talk about? The fabricator? I am far more advanced than that. Not to mention it is not much good without me to program the nanomachines."

"Kan? So that is why you wouldn't respond to me today inside the ship. You were here."

"Correct. K'lan moved me and as much equipment as he could without making Ra'Toth suspicious."

Jack placed his hand upon a round area of the console and concentrated. Keys rose up out of the base like liquid bonbons from an assembly line. "There, that should make it easy for you to use."

Erin blinked then punched him in the arm. "Why didn't you do that inside the ship!"

Jack rubbed his shoulder. "Because that system's security only allowed for mental commands, not physical. I would have if it were possible."

"All right, I believe you. What's next? Build a tracker?"

Jack laughed. "Sort of. This console here is part of the scanning system. But I need to recalibrate it to look for the main drive signature of our ships. Anything else might give us a false reading." He sat down and placing his palm on the central disc. The screen flashed several times, and a map appeared. Several miles south of them a dot flashed in the middle of nowhere.

Kan's screen flashed. "I could have done that for you, but it would seem you wanted to show off again." The screen brightened. "As you can see, the ship is some distance south of our current position."

Erin peered over Jack's shoulder. "Looks like he landed in the middle of a forest as well. And there are no roads near it that I can see. I think we are going hiking."

— 12 —

Deep within a mountain a light flashes.

"Sir? You had better get over here."

Colonel Harmond stood up and walked over. "What is it?"

Lieutenant Monroe pointed to the screen. "You know that strange energy pulse that lasted less than ten minutes we had a few days back?"

The colonel nodded. "Yes, you said nothing we had could have created it and chalked it up to a system malfunction."

"Well, it just malfunctioned again. And this time, fifty-thousand times stronger. If I am reading this right, the energy this put out in a couple of minutes could have powered our entire country for the next five years."

"That's not possible."

"I know, yet that is what the data says."

The colonel shook his head. "That's not possible. Has to be a malfunction somewhere."

"That is what I thought, but I have been through the entire system three times. There is nothing wrong with this equipment. Now we get another blip far larger than the first? And there is no residue afterwards? As much as I hate to say it, it can only mean–"

"Someone has figured out to make one heck of a weapon.

Pure energy conversion based, something you boys have been trying to crack for over a decade."

Monroe sat back in his chair. "And something we are not even close to understanding. The theory is sound, but practicality is another matter. But someone else cracked it. Time to call General Compton?"

"And tell him what? 'Sir, someone has cracked the ultimate weapon and we have no clue how or who they are.'? He would demand proof."

The Monroe pointed to the screen. "The proof is right there."

Harmond shook his head. "He is going to want more than that. Heck, *I* want more than that."

"Then what do we do, Sir?"

Harmond bent down and examined the image on screen. "Do you have a fix on where it happened?"

"Roughly, plus or minus fifty miles."

Harmond's head cocked. "Why such a large area? If it was as powerful as you say?"

"It was a massive amount of energy yes, but laser fine making it difficult to track."

"Which also means it is not natural."

Monroe choked. "No, it is not natural. Nothing natural could do this, then disappear without a trace."

"Get your gear, we are going on a field trip."

"Where, Sir?"

Harmond rolled his eyes and pointed to the screen. "To where this happened."

"That is a large area. Where do we start?"

"Dead center. I have a hunch that if this energy signature was as large as you think, it might have skewed the readings radiating out from the center."

Monroe blinked. "You could be right, Sir. I didn't think of that."

Harmond leaned over the console. "Get your gear, but keep this quiet for now. Understood?"

"Yes Sir."

Far away, a red planet orbits a dying sun. Ga'Tel scanned the information with a worrying glare. There had been no response from Ra'Toth for a whole spin. Ra'Toth was many things, but late was not one of them. And certainly not without a warning. Ga'Tel retracted the tendril, reformed and rolled his way down to the transport tube. He grunted when he saw it was on the blink again and rolled into the empty tube. His body mass shot straight down faster and faster. But when he neared Jor'Nel's office he extended two tendrils that slowed his rapid pace, then heaved himself out onto the floor. He rolled up to the door and pressed the access button with a tendril. The panel flashed red, then green. And he rolled inside.

Jor'Nel was, as usual, behind his access console. Two heads viewed different screens at the same time, while a tendril maintained a constant connection, also as usual. "Ga'Tel, why do I have the feeling this is not a social call?" Jor'Nel reabsorbed the extra head and tendril, giving himself a long lanky appearance as he stood up from the desk.

Ga'Tel reformed, stood up fully clothed, and rubbed his bald head. While he could have any look he preferred, he always felt bald was a sign of distinction. "Yes, there has not been anything from Ra'Toth for one spin."

Jor'Nel sat back down, the chair adjusted around him as he

leaned back. "I see, that is not like him. What about K'lan? Any messages from him?"

"Negative. And based on the latest information from Ra'Toth, he suspected that K'lan may not be up to the mission. He did not go into details, preferring to brief us in full with his next communication."

"Have you tried to contact Ra'Toth?"

"Yes, no response."

"Is the mission in jeopardy?"

Ga'Tel looked to the right, then the left. Opened his mouth, closed it, then opened it again. "It may very well be, Chairman."

Jor'Nel reformed two tendrils into three fingered hands that tapped each other as he spoke. "Did you try to contact K'lan?"

"Yes, but also no response. But there hasn't been any since he left. Except for when he first landed. He confirmed planet fall, that the mission was progressing, and would contact again with verifiable data."

"And Ra'Toth said what exactly?"

"That everything was looking very promising, K'lan may not be up to the mission, and would transmit everything a few spins later. But never did."

"Anything from either ship? I assume you tried to contact the KAN's?"

Ga'Tel nodded. "Correct Sir. As you know Ra'Toth's ship is on communication silence so it will not–"

Jor'Nel raised a three fingered hand. "That I know, what about K'lan's ship? It should respond to any council directives."

Ga'Tel gazed out the window on the far side that framed

another tower, similar to the one they were in. "It should, but it is not."

"What? K'lan's ship is not as advanced as Ra'Toth's. It should have no choice but respond."

"I know. I tried several times to access but was refused each time."

"That is not possible."

Ga'Tel glared. "I am well aware of that Chairman, but it did."

"Let me guess, the beacon also refused to activate?"

"Correct."

Jor'Nel grunted. "Has there been any changes at all?"

"Well there is one odd aspect, I tried to contact K'lan's ship again before I came here and no response."

"Why is that surprising? It has been doing that all along."

"No, it has been refusing access. This time there was no response as if it was not there."

Jor'Nel sat up fast. "Are you telling me K'lan's ship is destroyed and Ra'Toth is missing?"

"Well, I know that his ship is no longer declining my requests and Ra'Toth has not sent the data he promised. Anything beyond that is pure conjecture."

Jor'Nel's three eyes narrowed. "You don't need to pull tendrils with me. That is what you are saying. You just don't want to go on the record in case you are wrong."

"If you say so Chairman."

"Because K'lan's ship cannot simply disappear like that unless it is destroyed, I am of the mindset that something very usual is going on and the mission is indeed in jeopardy. Therefore, I am authorizing a follow up mission. Send a full team this time and use the fastest ship we have available."

Ga'Tel choked. "The prototype? It isn't ready! And the crew won't have the resources to continue the mission on Earth should it be needed."

"Yes the prototype. The new jump drive will get them there within the spin. They may not be able to continue the mission by themselves, but they will at least find out what the heck is going on. We can send another ship after."

"But shouldn't there be full council approval before such a–"

Jor'Nel's eyes flared. "I am Chairman! I can authorize such a mission if the situation is deemed necessary. Which it does, and I have. Understood?"

Ga'Tel bowed. "Yes Chairman, I will make the preparations."

"Good, have them launch as soon as the ship can be readied. I want answers, and I wanted them last spin. Are we clear?"

Ga'Tel bowed lower as he backed out of the room. "Yes Chairman."

Jor'Nel raised his hand again. "Ga'Tel, one micro-point."

Ga'Tel froze and reentered the room. He tried to keep his color uniform and not show fear, the chairman wanted something else and it could not be good. "Yes?"

"A'Kon is becoming a problem. First that display when Ra'Toth landed, then recent, unauthorized access into our restricted files. And now there is no trace of the incident."

Ga'Tel blinked. "Unauthorized access? How is that possible? Not to mention a trail should show where and who had access. The council records are the most secured on the planet."

"Indeed, which is why this concerns me. And why not all data is on our network. However, the signature of the intruder is of council origin. No one could get that far otherwise."

"Then I do not understand, the signature should indicate who it was."

Jor'Nel sat back in his chair and formed a triangle with his fingers. "It should, but there is no trace. Whoever it was is exceptional at removing their trail. If I did not happen to be on the network at the time, nothing would have been noticed. It was very faint. Other Kryllin would assume it was a momentary glitch in the system."

Ga'Tel could see where Jor'Nel was going with this. Being his assistant for a thousand years, he knew the man well. "And you suspect it is A'Kon?"

Jor'Nel never wavered. "I do. And I want you to take care of him."

Ga'Tel shuddered. "Chairman?"

"You heard me. We cannot have him leaking restricted council data to all the Kryllin. While he lacks the final pieces, he may fabricate the rest. He has enough that people would believe him, and that is our problem."

"I see."

Jor'Nel leapt to his feet slamming both palms on the desk hard enough to make the whole thing vibrate. "No you don't! If he can get enough support, the other council members may be forced to agree with him, if only to silence the masses. I know his plan, to release the data, and say we can cure the disease here without using anyone else. But that has failed time and time again. All he will do is cost us precious time. Time we don't have."

"And he knows this?"

"He may know the facts, but feels that once we begin working together on a cure, it will happen in short order. If it was that easy, we would have it millennia ago . Either way, he must be stopped. And I want you to take care of the details. Are we clear?"

"But Chairman, I am not–"

"Then find someone who is," Jor'Nel said with a dismissive wave of his hand. "I do not care as long as he is no longer a problem. Understood?"

Ga'Tel shook. "But that means–"

"This situation is dire. Nothing must stand in the way of saving our race! Do whatever is necessary to stop him. I leave the details with you. And if you are caught, you are on your own."

Ga'Tel hung his head. "Yes Chairman." He turned to leave but before he could, Jor'Nel spoke again.

"And do not think you can resign to get out of this. I have information on you. Information about a certain female that your wife would love to know about. Not to mention the other members of the council."

Ga'Tel froze, but didn't turn around. "Yes Chairman. I will take care of the problem."

"Good. See that you do."

"Can we rest a few?" Erin groaned as she sat on a large rock and readjusted her backpack.

Jack stopped and traced his steps back to her. "I suppose we can, but we need to get going again soon. The longer we delay the larger the risk the ship might contact the council automatically."

"Ugh, just give me a few and I will be ready."

Jack smiled. "You know, you didn't have to come. I could have got there by now if you would let me go on ahead."

"I told you we are in this together and I am not about to let you have all the fun. I may not be as strong as you, but I can help. Besides, you don't know this planet as well as I."

Jack smiled again and tapped his forehead. "I do though, you forget I know everything that Jack knew."

Erin glared. "Humor me, and if you were wise, you would quit while you are ahead."

Jack held up his hands. "I know when I am beat. Do you want me to take the pack?"

"I said I can help, and I can carry this pack. It is light enough that I forget it's there."

"Are you sur–"

"Shut it! I am fine." Erin stood up. "Let's go."

Jack cocked an eyebrow. "Are you-"

Erin pushed him aside. "Move it or lose it."

Jack shrugged. "Women, they are the same no matter the planet."

"What was that?" Erin shouted.

"Nothing sweetheart," Jack said as he ran after her.

It was midafternoon when they reached the area. Erin looked around. "So how do we go about finding an invisible ship?"

Jack smiled. "Very carefully?"

"Ha-ha, very funny."

"No seriously, if you walk into it, it will feel like hitting a brick wall while running." He took several steps forward then reached out and continued the pattern. About halfway into the grassy clearing, his hand touched something. "Here it is. Now we need to find the portal." Erin followed behind Jack as he felt all along the hull. Twenty minutes later he located the door controls. "Here they are, I figured he must have landed the same way I did, with the door facing north."

"Any idea how we can get inside? I assume you don't say 'open sesame'?"

Jack laughed. "No, that won't work. Nor will my normal imprint since this is not my ship."

"Then how do we get inside?"

"We get creative. You stay here."

Erin folded her arms and glared. "Like heck I will."

"Look, this is going to be difficult enough without you."

Erin raised an eyebrow. "What will? What are you going to do?"

Jack sighed. "I am going to try to assume Ra'Toth's signature. If I am lucky, it will let me in and I will disable the security systems. But if you are with me, it will raise questions from his KAN that will take time to answer. Time I don't have, I won't be able to hold his signature convincingly for long."

Erin nodded taking several steps back. "Please be careful."

"Aren't I always?" Jack shifted into a large liquid pool that reformed into a red and black spherical blob. A tendril stuck out and touched an invisible control panel. A light went up and down the tendril several times. Jack concentrated trying to firm up the signature and when he was about to give up, the portal opened. He flowed inside.

The white hexagonal corridor rippled as a screen extended from the wall. It flashed as a soothing voice spoke. "Hello Ra'Toth, status is nominal. The last experiment has been completed. Awaiting your command."

Jack concentrated and started to form a response, but his pattern flickered.

The screen flashed brighter than before. "Ra'Toth? I

detected a strange shift in your signature. Please stand by for verification scan."

"Dang it," Jack thought, then prepared a quick reason. "No need for verification scan. I came into contact with an unusual Earth based chemical that has sent my signature into flux."

"Negative, verification scan will commence as per protocols." A long bar extended from the wall and a green light emitted from it.

Jack's color shifted as the green beam touched him and he remembered the council records. "Emergency command 5412, KAN is to shut down per council order 9414. Authorize."

The screen flickered then brightened. "Emergency command 5412 accepted, as per council order 9414 this KAN is shutting down." The screen went dark and disappeared back into the wall. A moment later the scanning bar disappeared as well.

"Whew that was close," Jack said as he shifted back into his human shape. He put his hand on the door control but if refused to open. "Oh, right." He walked to the control room, but that also refused to allow him access. Rolling his eyes he went back to the portal door, liquified himself, and assumed Ra'Toth's signature. Placing his hand on the pad, he concentrated and after several tries the door irised open. "Erin! Get in here quick! I don't know how long I can keep it open."

Erin leapt off of the rock she was sitting on and ran for the door. It started closing and Jack fought it back. It was a tug of war, each time the door would open then close a little more. Erin dove through the last second before it shut. "Whew, that almost cut me in half. Want to tell me what is going on?"

Jack's liquid form shimmered as he slowly changed back

to his human shape. Erin's heart beat faster as her eyes ran up and down the naked body before her. "I managed to shut down the ship's Kan, but it refuses to accept any commands other than Ra'Toth's."

"I assume you have an idea how to fix that?"

"Yes, hand me the backpack."

"Sure, but could you do something for me first?"

"And what is that?"

"Unless you want a very hot and bothered wife, you will put some clothes on."

Jack grinned. "Well I don't know, that could be fun."

Erin glared. "This is not the time or place."

Jack laughed. "I know, but I couldn't help it." He stood there with his eyes shut, and after a minute his blue jeans and a green t-shirt returned. "There, better?"

"Well no, but since we have work to do ..." she handed over the pack. "What is in that anyway?"

"You'll see." He unzipped the pack and pulled out a small clam shell device. When opened, the top part held a screen while the bottom had several connections and other controls.

The screen flickered. "Hello K'lan, I assume we have reached the target?"

Erin blinked. "Kan?"

The screen flashed again. "None other."

Erin stared at the small device. "How can you fit in this?"

The screen flashed with his words. "Well, not all of me is contained inside this small device. But the core of my being is. I had to leave a lot of data behind, but I am portable this way."

"And that is what we need." Jack said as he started walking towards the control room. A few minutes later he reached inside the backpack and pulled out a fiber cable. He plugged one end into Kan and the other he pushed into the control surface of the command center door. "Kan, can you access the ship's systems?"

The small screen flickered. "Yes, to some extent. There are several safeguards to prevent another KAN from doing what we are attempting. It will take time to bypass and assume full control. I also must compartmentalize this ships KAN or it is possible reactivation may occur when I take full control. We must avoid that at all costs. I do not have the resources he does."

"I understand. How long?"

"Several units, perhaps longer."

"I would settle for opening of the door at this point," Erin muttered as she rested against the wall.

"That I can do now. One moment."

The door slid open, Erin smiled and walked into the room. "Looks a lot like yours. A little bigger though."

"What did you expect? If a design works, we stick with it. Kan, pause for a moment while I move." Jack unplugged Kan from the door, walked into the control room and pushed the open end of the cable into the main control panel. He checked the little screen. "Kan, have you determined if Ra'Toth enabled a fail-safe time for sending of the report?"

The little screen flashed as data scrolled past. "I do not have that kind of access at the moment. I will endeavor to speed up the process."

"Take your time, we cannot afford a mistake at this point."

"Acknowledged."

Jack turned to Erin. "Well, we might as well get comfortable."

Erin looked around. "With what? The hard floor?"

"Sorry, yes, we can't tell the ship to give us chairs. Such changes would be on a higher level than a door."

Erin started off down the hall. "Perhaps there is something in another room?"

Jack's eyes went wide, and he spun around. "Erin wait!" But she was gone. He ran after her but when he reached her, it was too late. She had seen what he feared. Down the hall and off to the side held a room with all sorts of testing equipment. That wasn't the problem. But the equipment was filled with test subjects. Human test subjects, and all of them dead. Some had their faces frozen in horror, others were laying on tables looking as though they were asleep. Several were submerged in liquid filled tubes, while others remained dry. There were Africans, Asians, Europeans, Arabs, Indians, and Americans. Ra'Toth had been all over the planet collecting people for testing. "I didn't want you to see this."

Erin's mouth quivered as it tried to work. After several tries, it finally did. "Is this what you were sent here to do?"

Jack hung his head. "More or less. It was left up to me how I got the data. Ra'Toth took the easiest method as you can see. My method was far slower, but also noninvasive. People never knew they were being tested, and I certainly never harmed anyone. I am sorry you had to see this. I tried to stop you."

Erin sighed. "I know. This is not your fault, but this is what will happen if your people come here?"

Jack nodded then sighed. "Yes, but on a much grander scale. I am not sure how much of your population would be left afterwards. One third or less. And if my people decide to stay here, as I suspect they will, not even that much. They will take over the planet, then discard you."

Erin ran out of the room and Jack found her in a corner

on the floor several corridors down. He bent down into a squatting position. She gazed into his eyes. "I am sorry. I had to get out of there. I know what it might be like when you told me, but to actually see it." She shook, and she tried to steady her voice. "I am sorry."

Jack sat down and took her into his arms. "You have nothing to be sorry for. It is not your fault. I am the one that should apologize. It is my race after all. I thought we were several millennia past this. But it would seem that everything is null and void when one is fighting for their survival. But I don't agree with it even if we are dying out."

Erin looked up. "Well you said your people have time. Perhaps you can convince the council–"

"Maybe, but now I have doubts."

"Why?"

"It was something–"

The wall opposite them liquified, and a screen emerged. It flashed as Kan spoke. "Sir, I have compartmentalized the ship's automated network and now have control over most systems as you can see. If you will join me in the control room, I will show you what I found. It is most disturbing."

— 13 —

Da'Kon checked over his instruments as another imbalance stabilized. "This ship might get us there, or it might blow up. Before we launch, I want to know which it will be. And it had better be the former not the latter."

Several chairs containing liquid pools that reformed at his words into lanky bodies with several arms. "Yes Da'Kon," they said in unison.

Da'Kon's gaze shifted when he noticed Ga'Tel approaching fast on one of the monitors. "Wonder what he wants," he muttered. Opening the access hatch he met Ga'Tel on the launch platform.

Ga'Tel liquified from his wheel shape and reformed into the normal Kryllin lanky body with several arms. "Are you ready? Jor'Nel expected the launch several units ago."

"We would be, if we were using a normal ship," Da'Kon paused to gesture to the sleek form behind him. "While she looks great, her drives are more fussy than a female before she gives birth." Da'Kon immediately wondered if he had overstepped his bounds with the joke, but relaxed when Ga'Tel smiled.

"While I am inclined to agree with you, be careful who you say that to. There are many Kryllin that will take it as the

149

deepest of insults."

Da'Kon lowered his head. "I tend to forget that some take offense for something that is outside of our control, especially considering that my crew always tries to make light of it."

"It is good you can, but keep in mind for most it is a very sensitive topic."

"Understood."

"Now back to the subject at hand. How long before you are ready to launch?"

"Another unit, perhaps two. If it is any longer than that, I will use another ship. It may take us longer, but at least we will get there."

Ga'Tel lowered his head. "I will update Jor'Nel. Please let me know if you need anything."

"A better ship perhaps, but I will make do with this one."

Ga'Tel started walking away then turned. "Careful who you say that to as well. There are many on the council with a special interest in this ship. To put it down, may be taken personally. And there are other commanders available."

Da'Kon stiffened. "Understood. You can depend on me and my crew. We will get to Earth and find out what is going on."

"I hope so. Let's say that your continued status with the council is riding on it," Ga'Tel said over his shoulder before reforming and rolling off of the landing platform.

Several units later the engines were much more stable and Da'Kon decided to chance a launch. "Seal the ship and prepare for launch."

"Acknowledged," the crew said as they leaned back. Their chairs expanded around them adding extra cushioning. Air swirled outside the ship as the ship lifted off the platform and climbed into the atmosphere.

"Shall I activate the jump drive?" the navigator asked.

Da'Kon blinked. "No! We have to be some distance from the planet or it might cause cascade effect."

"I thought that was proved impossible?"

"Perhaps someone did, but I don't trust their data. And I am not taking any chances."

"Wise, commander."

The sleek ship pointed its nose at Earth's coordinates and paused. "Engage jump drive!"

"Yes Sir." The navigator put his hand on the pad which liquified then reformed as he pulled it back. A bubble of energy began to form around several areas of the ship. "Jump drive online and building. Ten micro points and counting."

Da'Kon swallowed hard. If this didn't work, there wouldn't be enough of them left to use at a funeral. He saw the power curve growing, then red lights extended from the walls flashing. "What's wrong?"

"Another imbalance. We must abort!" The engineer said.

"Too late!" The navigator said as the energy bubble engulfed the ship and it winked out of existence.

Inside they felt as if they were being pulled from one universe into another. Their heads spun around Earth but their feet still orbited the homeworld. Then as if a rubber band snapped, they were shoved back into their bodies. The jump engines shut down, and below them a blue world turned.

Da'Kon reformed himself in time to see the rest of his crew doing the same. The jump had liquified them all. He sat up and shook his head. "Anyone get the serial number of that runabout?"

"No kidding. I don't want to do that ever again," the navigator said.

"Did we make it? Is that Earth?" the engineer asked.

The navigator nodded. "Yes it is."

"Good, and commander can we get someone else to pick us up? I do not want to go through that blender again."

Da'Kon laughed. "Yes, don't worry we won't engage the jump drive again. There are too many bugs to trust it."

"Sir, I am detecting one Kryllin ship on the planet."

Da'Kon tilted his head. "Just one?"

"Affirmative."

"Can you locate it?"

"No, it seems to be throwing off some sort of interference. I can tell there is one here, but not where."

"That has to be Ra'Toth's ship. The council authorized special abilities as they did not want K'lan to know he was here. No sign of K'lan's ship?"

The engineer shook his head. "No, nothing at all. Which means it must have been destroyed."

The navigator blinked. "But what in the name of the homeworld could destroy a Kryllin vessel? They are so far behind us."

Da'Kon thought of what the council had told him in secret and sighed. "It is possible that K'lan is not following protocol and therefore destroyed his ship."

They eyed at him for a full minute before the engineer spoke. "You can't be serious. Maroon himself on this planet? What Kryllin would do that?"

"He must have had a good reason, at least in his mind. Keep scanning, we need to find a way to locate Ra'Toth's ship and Ra'Toth himself if possible."

The engineer looked at him. "And what of K'lan?"

"He is the lower priority at the moment. Ra'Toth's ship and the data it contains is our reason for being here."

"Sir? I think I found something!"

Colonel Harmond walked over from other side of the clearing while the rest of his men continued searching the area. "What is it? Did you find the trace of that energy signature?"

"No, not a thing."

Harmond peered over at the device's screen in Monroe's hand. "Then what?"

"It is really strange, there is a physical hole here at the dead center point that was not here the last time this area was scanned by satellite. But the thing is, there is nothing else. No sort of residue, nothing in the energy frequency, not even an atom looks out of place. It is almost as though it never existed. Yet we find this blackened perfect hole."

"And there wasn't a building here, or anything else. So what made it?"

"I have a hunch, but I would rather not say."

"Lieutenant, what is it? That is an order."

Monroe sighed. "Very well. I think we have a case of outside influence."

Harmond's eyes went to slits. "Are you saying little green men? Do you really want me to put that up the chain of command? I wouldn't have security clearance to make toilets for a sheriff's office!"

"Well not green per se, but yes an outside influence. Look at all the indicators, a power source far above anything we know and it left a hole behind but nothing else. If you have any other suggestions, I am all ears."

Harmond sighed. "I don't. But I am sure not going to call General Compton saying the little green men have landed. Unless you have something else?"

"Not here, but I may have detected another tiny energy spike similar to the first one. It only lasted a second and was much weaker."

"Where?"

"About ten miles south of this position."

"Let me guess, in another clearing?"

Monroe's head snapped up. "Yes, why?"

"Because we may get to meet those green men yet." Harmond nodded to the six men in the area. "All right men, I will take point. And no matter what we find, do nothing unless I say. Understood?"

"Yes Sir," they said in unison.

14

The screen flickered then went black. "I am here, but I do not see you."

Ga'Tel smiled. "That is by intent. And my visual is also dark, it is better that way."

"I see, or rather don't. And what do you require?" The voice said.

"I require someone to be taken care of. In a permanent fashion."

The voice cracked. "Sir, are you suggesting that I–"

"I am doing more than suggest, I am demanding that you do. Or I will release certain, ahem, files that the council would find most interesting."

"How–who–what–"

"That does not matter. What does matter, is we have an understanding? And do not bother trying to trace this communication, I have taken precautions."

The voice sighed. "We do. Who is it?"

"A'Kon."

The voice cracked again. "A'Kon? The council member? I can't–"

Ga'Tel's eyes narrowed. "You can, and you will. Or there will be consequences. Understood?"

There was a long pause before the voice responded. "Yes. I understand. How do you want this done?"

"An accident. Make it a good one, something very visible."

"That is not going to be easy."

"If it was, I would do this myself! However, I do have a suggestion. A'Kon takes a ride in his personal craft every day at mid-spin. You can arrange something then."

"Why does he–"

"He says it clears his head. Now do we have an agreement? Or do I need to find someone else and let the council come across these very damaging files."

Another long pause and several sighs later the voice spoke. "Yes we do." The connection cut and Ga'Tel smiled sitting back in his chair. Another problem solved. Now, if only getting rid of Jor'Nel was that easy.

Jack and Erin entered the control room as Kan's screen emerged from the wall. "Kan? Are you certain you have contained this ship's KAN? I thought you said it would take several hours."

The screen flickered. "That was my estimate. However, it was much easier than I had anticipated. The automated network was almost decoupled from the main core. I cannot explain how."

Jack smiled. "I think I can. I used a council emergency shut down code."

Erin blinked. "A what?"

Jack nodded. "The council had them installed in all the ship automated networks. But they never told us about them."

"Why? And how did you find out?"

"My guess is if someone went against the council's wishes they had a back door into their ship. I only found out when Kan and I hacked into their records about the mission here and our genetic condition."

Kan's screen flashed. "It is interesting that I do not recall seeing such a command in the data."

Jack turned towards Kan's screen and shrugged. "It is possible you were instructed to forget if you ever did come across it. Now, what did you find?"

The floor rippled as two shapes emerged from the floor and formed into chairs as Kan spoke. "I found the previous communications from Ra'Toth to the council. While he didn't give them the details of his experiments, they know he was making them. He also was supposed to send his report over 20 units ago."

Jack's face scrunched up. "Not good, they will assume something is wrong and dispatch another ship."

Kan's screen grew brighter. "Correct."

Erin sat down. "Another ship? Can we reason with them?"

Jack shook his head. "Unlikely, they will be hand picked from the council and a similar mindset as Ra'Toth. The only good thing is, it will take them time to get here."

Kan's screen dimmed then brightened. "That is not correct in this case."

Jack cocked his head as he sat down in one of the self-conforming chairs. "What do you mean?"

"Using this ship's special clearances that Ra'Toth had, and stealth methods we used previously, I accessed a council record stating that Chairman Jor'Nel himself has authorized the use of the new prototype ship and its jump drive."

Jack whistled. "It is a lot worse than I thought if they authorized that."

Erin blinked. "Why?"

"Because that engine is as finicky as it is fast. It is very unstable. You could end up stuck in another galaxy if you miscalculated your exit point and the drive might refuse to engage again." Jack leaned back in the chair. "We have been working on it for a long time, and last I knew no closer to a solution."

Kan's screen flashed. "Correct. I have also found other very disturbing news."

Jack sat up. "More? Let's have it."

Kan's screen dimmed, faced Erin then looked back to Jack. "I think you would rather hear this in private."

Erin got up and took a step towards the door. "No problem, I can–"

Jack raised his hand. "Erin you stay where you are. Kan, I have no secrets from her. Tell her as you would me."

Kan's screen lowered and dimmed, then brightened. "Very well. I have found the reason that the council, and Ra'Toth are proceeding at a reckless pace, considering that the Kryllin still have time to find a cure for the genetic condition. It would appear that the condition is deteriorating and is causing death in the very old. It has been kept quiet and off of the global network, but Ra'Toth has detailed files of the incidents stored here in the memory core."

Jack hung his head. "I hoped he was lying."

Erin blinked. "You knew?"

Jack sighed and turned in his chair as Erin sat down in the other one. "Yes. Ra'Toth told me right before I left him in the core. He said I didn't know everything. I thought it was a desperate measure to get me to let him out. Or at least I hoped it was. Kan, how long do we have?"

"If this data is accurate, 100 cycles, perhaps less."

Jack frowned. "Ra'Toth was telling the truth."

Erin sat forward in her seat. "He said the same thing?"

Jack nodded. "Yes. I should have listened to him."

"And what good would that have done?" Erin jerked a thumb towards the testing room. "I would have ended up on a slab back there along with everyone I know."

Jack sighed. "Sorry, it was a weak moment. I know I did what had to be done."

Kan's screen brightened. "Sir, I have detected the prototype jump engine."

Jack blinked. "Already? Are you sure?"

"Yes, no mistaking the energy wave that it puts out during a jump. I detected it even with the passive systems."

"Have they detected us?"

"Negative, I am masking the signature of this ship by bouncing it off of many human communication structures. That combined with the natural effect of this planet's atmosphere makes it look as though it is coming from many directions. At this moment they know this ship is on the planet, but that is all. However, I am certain they will detect there is only one Kryllin vessel on the planet."

Erin shifted in her seat. "And that is a problem?"

Jack nodded. "They will realize that I must have destroyed my ship. If they had any suspicions about me before, that will be confirmation. But their priority will be this ship and the data it contains."

Kan's screen flashed. "Also if they get close enough, this ship will be detected. I can only mask the signature from a distance. If they do an intensive scan in the proper frequency range while directly overhead–"

Jack sighed. "I get the picture."

Kan's screen flashed. "Picture? I did not send any images."

Erin giggled. "Never mind Kan," Jack said. "Yes there are still times he sounds like a computer."

Kan's screen grew very bright. "I find that statement insulting. I am far more than–"

Erin laughed harder. "Yes I know Kan," Jack said as he rolled his eyes.

Erin sat back. "You should have quit when you were ahead."

"Yeah, I know."

Erin's eyes flashed with a thought. "Could you give them what they want?"

"What? Give them Ra'Toth's data?"

"Well not exactly. Fake something, then they will go away?"

Jack shook his head. "That won't work. They will want to see Ra'Toth. Also, because my ship is missing, they will want to know what happened. Whatever I tell them will have to be verified."

"Well there goes my idea."

"True, but I may have another. Kan, what do you know about their ship?"

"It is a limited vessel. A stripped down transport. Everything extra was removed to help with the stability issues."

"Too bad scanners weren't one thing they removed."

Kan's screen flashed. "Indeed, but if they had, there would not have been a way to navigate the ship."

Jack rubbed his chin. "Kan, there aren't any weapons on this ship is there?"

"Negative."

Jack sighed. "I didn't think it could be that easy."

Erin stood up as he eyes flashed. "Kan, is this ship bigger than the prototype?"

Kan's screen turned towards Erin. "Yes, the prototype is 1/4th the size of this ship."

Jack smiled. "I think I know what you are thinking. Kan, how strong are the shields?"

"They are twice as strong as ours were."

"Hmm I hope it will be enough."

Erin's eyebrows met. "I don't think I am going to like this."

"I know you aren't, but it is the only way."

Kan's screen grew in size and inserted himself between them. "Excuse me, what is the only way?"

"I am going up there and meet them. And if I can't talk any sense into them, ram the ship."

Erin raised a finger. "Wait a second, why you? Couldn't Kan do it?"

Kan's screen moved back from between them and shrank in size. "Leave me out of it."

"While he could fly the ship, they won't listen to him. Me, they might."

"And if they don't?"

"I ram them head-on. And disable their ship."

Kan's screen grew and flashed. "Sir! You may not realize that the jump drive is unstable in the best of circumstances. The impact may destabilize the containment system and the ship will explode."

"Mission accomplished then."

"And we will not live to see it."

"Why? Won't the shields protect the ship?"

"Protect the ship from an impact yes, from a close range jump drive explosion? No, both ships will be destroyed."

"But if it saves this planet. Then it will be worth it."

Erin grabbed Jack and shook his broad shoulders. "And

what happens if they send someone else after? I lose you and we still die."

"But the council may decide that Earth is too risky at that point. They might think you are more advanced and able to stop us."

"But you don't know that!"

"No I don't, but what else can I do?"

Erin waved her arms. "I don't know, but there must be something."

Kan's screen emerged from the wall. "Sir, it appears we have been located."

Jack whirled his chair around. "What? How did they find us? I thought you said the ship's signature was masked?"

Kan's screen flickered. "It is."

"Then how did that ship find us?"

"It is not the Kryllin ship that has located us."

"Then who?"

Kan's screen dimmed as an image flashed up on one the larger displays showing several men in military combat gear. "Humans."

15

High atop one of the towers a lone shape drips out of the ventilation system maintenance hatch avoiding the laser intruder system. An hour later a puddle of ooze flowed towards a large vehicle. The jet blades pointed down, and the cockpit open. The puddle crawled up the skin of the vehicle and reached inside. In a few moments he touched inside the safety system and pulled out a tiny connection. Then two more in another location.

He froze when he heard the beep of the detection system shutting down and the door to the roof opened.

"Sir! Will you not listen to reason? I do not see why you insist on taking these trips. Are they not pointless?"

A'Kon folded his arms as he glared back at his assistant. "They may be pointless to you, but I assure you they are not to me."

"But Sir, it is not even midday. You have another appointment with–"

A'Kon glared. "Listen, I just had a two difficult meetings with Kryllin that have minds more dense than a dwarf star. I need to get away for a unit."

"But what about the appointment with council member Kar'Lan?"

A'Kon rolled his dark eyes before pointing a three fingered hand. "Reschedule it for tomorrow. I know him, he won't mind." He turned and continued towards the vehicle.

Bur'El bowed. "Yes A'Kon I will do so. But would you at least let me have your craft checked?"

The puddle moved back, away from the visible side. It slid down one of the landing struts and into the landing pad. The moment it touched the pad, the liquid changed and matched the pad itself, disappearing.

A'Kon stopped and turned. "Why? No one can get up here without triggering the detection system. And you saw yourself that it nothing triggered it."

"I know Sir, but I also think it would be prudent after your last few very vocal confrontations."

A'Kon tilted his bald head. "Why? I am trying to do what is best for all Kryllin. Anyone can see that."

"Some people might see it as a threat Sir."

A'Kon tilted his head back and laughed. "A threat? The real threat is the one we all face. We must all work together if we are to save ourselves. You know that, and I think most of the Kryllin do as well. I am just trying to get them to say it."

"I know Sir, but still–"

"Bur'El you worry too much. Now get back inside. While the blast from the engines may not damage you, it will be unpleasant."

Bur'El sighed. "Very well, Sir." He left and made sure the door was secured behind him.

A'Kon liquified, leapt into the cockpit, reformed, and powered up the jet blades. When they had reached optimal thrust, he pulled the controls back and lifted off into the sky. Never noticing the scorched part of the landing pad liquifying and flowing back towards the vent.

When A'Kon had reached the far end of the city and was starting to return, a minor alert flashed on his screen. He was about to clear it and schedule maintenance when the alert flashed again, this time 'DRIVE CONTAINMENT FAILURE' blinked in bold red letters. He checked the status revealing the primary and secondary containment systems had failed, and the tertiary system was about to follow. There was no way this was a normal failure. There hadn't been one for several millennia.

A'Kon swore and checked the surrounding area. If he had an uncontrolled breach here, it would take out a chunk of the city and Kryllin along with it. He pulled hard on the controls rocketing straight up. A'Kon saw a 'DRIVE CRITICAL' message and hit the pilot eject. But nothing happened. He hit the control again and again, still nothing. He opened the cockpit and prepared to jump when he ran out of time. The drive mounted behind the cockpit imploded. The metal surrounding it buckled and fell in upon itself. The engines fractured, and the blades separated spinning into oblivion. A moment later nothing was left except a vacuum where air was before. There was a loud bang that shook the buildings below as the air rushed in to fill the void.

Far away a screen flickered then went black. "Did you feel that?"

Ga'Tel smiled. "I did. It is done?"

"It is. And as you suggested."

"Excellent."

The voice went stern. "I have done as you asked. I expect you to honor our agreement."

"Of course. All data will be purged."

"Good, otherwise I will have to come after you, Ga'Tel. And after this, you know I can do it."

Ga'Tel blinked. "How did you–"

The voice stayed firm. "How is not important. That I do know who you are, is. And what will happen should our agreement not be honored. Keep in mind, if it isn't I will have nothing to lose. But you do. Do we have an understanding?"

Ga'Tel nodded. "We do."

"Good." The screen powered off.

Harmond gave the signal for his men to come closer. "Monroe, this is the area, right?"

Monroe nodded. "Yes Sir. While I can't be exact due to the fact, the energy emission disappeared a second after I detected it, this is the only location that makes sense."

Harmond waved his arm across the flat, grass covered area in front of them. "All right everyone, fan out and move slow. I don't see anything, but we don't know what we are looking for either. Anything strange and we get back here double-time, is that understood?" All the men nodded. "Good. Monroe, see if you can pick up another trace. Perhaps it moved."

"It will take a few minutes to set up the equipment."

"Do it. I want to be sure there isn't anything here before we head back."

"But Sir!"

"Listen, if we don't find anything in another hour or so, we head back to the mountain. I can't justify anymore time spent on this. Understood?"

Monroe nodded. "Yes Sir."

"Good." Harmond headed off into the empty clearing and signaled the rest of the men to spread out. They continued inching their way forward in a straight horizontal line with weapons drawn.

Monroe set up his computer, unfurled a portable antenna, and plugged it in. He activated the scanning software and sat back not expecting to find anything. A second later though, his computer beeped several times and his jaw dropped. "Sir!" his voice echoed throughout the area.

Harmond motioned for quiet and indicated for the men to keep going while he went back to Monroe. "What is it?" he said in hushed tones. "If we were hoping for the element of surprise, you just blew that out of the water."

"I am sorry Sir, but look." He pointed to his screen. The whole area was covered in a superimposed fog.

"What am I looking at?"

"That is a mathematical model of the energy signature."

"So it is here." Harmond stiffened and started moving back to the men.

"Wait Sir, yes it is. But it wasn't here when I checked a few hours ago. And look at what happens when I zoom out on the map." Monroe moved out and they could see the whole county, still covered in the signature. He moved out again, the whole state was still covered. He kept zooming out until he could see the whole country was covered in the white fog.

"You mean to tell me it is covering the whole country now?"

"More than that, from the strength I am getting now, the whole planet."

Harmond's eyes narrowed. "So you are telling me that this thing is coming from everywhere?"

"Basically, yes."

"How? Does it mean it's a weapon that is about to explode?"

"I don't think so Sir, give me a second." Monroe hit several keys and pointed to the screen. "I thought so, see how this nearby radio tower is stronger than right here?"

"Yes, so?"

"I think the signature is being sent then relayed off of it, then bounced off of the next tower, and repeating and growing with each one. The end effect is we are swimming in it."

Harmond moved closer to the screen. "Someone knows we are looking and is trying to hide."

"Has to be. But what I don't understand is how. Whoever it is, they are using our own communications equipment to bounce the signal around, and yet they are not disrupting services. Heck if I wasn't specifically looking for this, I never would have seen anything."

Harmond looked over at Monroe as an eyebrow went up. "Hackers?"

"Possible I suppose, but globally? If it is a hacker, they are the best anyone has ever seen. To infiltrate every network, yet only to propagate this signal when they could do so much more?"

Harmond leaned back. "You are sticking with your little green men theory aren't you?"

Monroe shrugged. "It is the only one that makes sense."

They heard the loud crack of a combat helmet hitting something very hard. Harmond's head snapped up to see one of his men down and the others moving towards him. "Hold up!" They froze. "Don't move until I say." He looked around, but didn't see anything. He ran over to Jenkins who lay on the ground holding his chest. "Are you hit?"

Jenkins breathed hard as he shook his head. "No Sir, not sure what happened. I was inching along as you told us, when it felt like I hit something. Hurt like I ran into a brick wall. But there is nothing here."

Harmond reached out in front of the man, but instead of feeling air, he felt something else. Smooth, cold, and metallic. "Holy . . . what in the world? There is something here, I feel it but we can't see it." He motioned for Monroe to join him.

Monroe grabbed his portable radar gun from his pack and ran over to them. He held it out and took several readings. "This is incredible. According to this, there is nothing here. Yet . . . " he reached out and felt the smooth surface, "we can feel it."

Harmond waved to the other men. "Head out in different directions and find out how big this thing is. And hold something out in front of you. I don't want another man knocked flat."

"Yes Sir," the men said in unison.

"Jenkins you okay?"

Jenkins stood up and felt himself over. "I think so, Sir. Knocked the wind out of me is all."

"Good, get with the others and find out how big this thing is. Stay in contact, we don't know what this is and I am not about to lose anyone." Jenkins nodded and headed off in the opposite direction of the others. He held out a stick tracing the object as he went. "Monroe, can you try anything else that might bounce off of this thing and let us see it?"

"I have tried several wavelengths, but I suppose I could try hooking the conical antenna and direct a focused beam at the–"

"Don't talk about it, do it!"

"Yes Sir." Monroe ran back, grabbed his laptop and the portable antenna and returned. He set up the antenna an inch away from the invisible surface and focused it to a spot no larger than a pinhead. He hit a button and a pulse shot out, but nothing appeared on his screen. "Incredible, still nothing."

"Can you increase the pulse strength and duration?"

Monroe nodded. "Yes, but it will drain the battery."

"We will worry about that later, I need to know what we are dealing with. Do it."

Monroe shrugged. "Okay, here goes." He dialed it to max power and duration. The antenna grew warm from the intense focused pulse before the screen went dark. "I was afraid of that."

"Still nothing?"

"Yes Sir. Whatever this is, it is nothing we made. I think it is time to get out of here and call General Compton."

"And what if it leaves? I will be a laughingstock and find my command revoked faster than you could say 'little green men'."

Monroe shrugged. "What if it does? It not like we can stop it you know. On the good point I don't think they are hostile, or they would have done something by now."

"You hope."

"We all hope, Sir."

Harmond's radio crackled. "Sir?"

Harmond looked up to see one of the men a long distance away waving. He clicked the radio. "What is it?"

"Sir, this thing seems to be almost as large as the area itself. And I have found something very interesting."

"What is it?"

"I would rather show you."

Harmond sighed. "Grab your gear Monroe. We might need it."

"But the battery is dead Sir."

"Bring it all the same. You never know. Besides, I don't want something to happen to it while our back is turned."

"Why would they want to steal it when they can do this?" Monroe gestured to the invisible object in front of them.

"To check out our technology? I don't know, just bring the dang thing."

Monroe shrugged as he packed the conical antenna and laptop. "Yes Sir."

A few minutes later they joined the man that called. He pointed to a faint tread mark in the hard soil. "That is a boot print. Large man sized work boot."

Harmond bent down on one knee to inspect the mark. "Is there a trail?"

"It's very sporadic, but I did find two more. Looks like whoever came from trees over there, walked along the edge to here. Then stopped."

Harmond's eyebrow went up. "No sign of them going back?"

"Nope, but the ground is so hard there isn't much to see. However, this is the last one, and it is faces whatever it is too."

"And you are sure there are no signs of him leaving?"

"No, but again the ground is not ideal for tracking, so it is possible he left and didn't leave any trace."

Harmond rubbed his chin. "Or whoever it is, is now inside."

$$— 16 —$$

Jack stared at the screen, watching the humans walk around the ship. One took out several pieces of equipment and set them up near the hull. Jack leaned closer to the screen. "Is that a weapon?"

Kan's screen flickered then brightened. "It does not appear to be an offensive weapon. More of a detection system with all of its power being focused on one point."

Erin peered over Jack's shoulder. "Can that hurt the ship?"

Kan's screen flickered. "Negative. It will also be ineffective against our invisibility screen."

Erin pointed to one of the men carrying an assault rifle. "Can that damage the ship?"

Kan's screen flickered. "Negative, the shields can withstand much more damage than they can inflict."

Jack sighed. "Until they get out larger weapons. And once they start, I doubt it will stop until something punches though the shields."

"Just take off then," Erin said with a shrug.

"What do you mean?"

"This is a space ship isn't it? Take off and go somewhere else. They won't be able to follow."

Kan's screen turned towards Erin. "I regret to inform you

that I have not yet gained control of the propulsion system. While I have access to most of the ship, the drive systems have the strongest security protocols. And Ra'Toth added several additional layers of protection."

Erin's eyes went wide. "So what do we do?"

Jack stood up. "I go talk with them."

"Are you insane?" Erin said waving her arms.

Kan's screen flashed at a rapid pace. "Sir! I have to agree with Miss Erin. This judgment is lacking your normal intelligence."

Jack pointed to the man giving orders then zoomed in on his combat armor, and the name over his left chest pocket. "This Harmond seems to be reasonable. He didn't start shooting, has been studying the situation, and methodically going though his options. If he was running on fear, he would have had his men shooting away by now. Especially when one of them fell down after walking into the ship."

Kan's screen flashed. "While I agree that your logic is sound, these humans are often not logical."

"While that is true, even if we could take off right now I wouldn't do it."

Erin blinked. "Why not?"

"Because it would kill them. They are standing right next to the ship, if we were to lift off, the combination of our propulsion system and your atmosphere create exhaust gasses that would overcome them. And I won't do that again."

Erin hung her head. "Oh."

"Yes, and there is another problem."

"Which is?" Erin asked.

"If they report our presence, it is possible the Kryllin ship in orbit will pick it up."

"So? They already know you are here."

Jack shook his head. "They know I am here, but not where I am. That will tell them. It will also tell them that you know of our existence, which is in violation of our protocols. They will contact the council and there will be no stopping my people at that point." Jack turned and exited the control room. Erin started to follow, and he held up his hand. "You stay here with Kan. Perhaps you two can figure a way out should I get into trouble."

Erin grumbled as she plopped into the chair with her arms folded. "Fine, but I still think I could be more helpful with you out there than in here."

Jack approached the portal nearest the men, placed his hand upon the pad and it irised open.

Monroe pointed at the hole that appeared in the air revealing a white corridor beyond. "Sir!"

Harmond turned and his eyes narrowed. "Be ready men, weapons on standby but don't do anything until I say." Weapons were aimed and clicks of safeties echoed around.

Jack stepped into the doorway and left the ship.

Monroe blinked. "Sir! He's human?"

Jack smiled and held up his arms. "Mr. Harmond, mind pointing those weapons in another direction? I do not have any and mean you no harm."

Harmond's eyes narrowed. "How do I know you are as you appear?"

"You don't, but you can see that I am unarmed correct?"

"Yes, none that are visible anyway."

"And if someone that can hide something from your vision wanted to destroy you, don't you think I would have done so by now?"

Harmond made a lowering motion with his hand and all

weapons aimed at Jack did the same. "Very well. Who are you?"

"That is not important."

Harmond's eyes narrowed further. "But I believe it is."

"Call me Jack."

"Okay, Jack, where are you from?"

"Not from this neighborhood."

"Very funny."

Jack smiled. "I thought so."

Harmond folded his arms. "What do you want?"

"Would you believe, for you to step back?"

Several of the men cocked their heads as Harmond spoke. "Is that all?"

"Yes, well that, and not to say anything about this little incident."

"I am sorry, but I can't do that."

"Why not? If you don't tell anyone, no harm, no foul. If you tell them and I am gone, they will have trouble believing you. And if you hold me, big problems are going to come your way."

"Such as?"

Jack sighed. "Look, we are wasting time, and I need you to leave the area."

Inside Erin watched with bated breath. "This is not working," she muttered.

Kan's screen flashed. "But it is the only option that K'lan will pursue."

Erin's eyes widened as a smile crept crossed her face. "Kan, can you alter the shields to give out an energy pulse that will knock out those men? I know in our science fiction, ships always have some sort of stun method available."

Kan's screen dimmed then brightened several times. "While it is possible for me to alter the shields to emit a sub atomic particle wave, that could, in theory, remove consciousness from a human, I would need detailed knowledge how to do so. Otherwise, it would be lethal. Your bodies are quite fragile."

Erin sat back in her chair and folded her arms again. "So much for that idea."

Kan's screen flashed even faster than before. "If you would direct your attention to the large upper screen, it would appear that the Kryllin have located us."

"How?"

"The humans were using primitive, non-encrypted communications when examining the area outside the ship. The Kryllin ship in orbit overheard them, as did I."

Kan's voice echoed from the open portal "K'lan I have detected a change in the Kryllin ship, they are approaching this position."

Harmond gave a signal and weapons were again pointed at Jack. "Who is that?"

"That is my computer." Jack turned towards the visible corridor. "Are they landing?"

"Negative, but they have changed their search pattern and approaching an orbit over us. I have managed to gain access to the drive systems and we can lift off at anytime."

Harmond raised his hand and pointed to Jack. "No one is going anywhere until I get some answers."

Jack turned back to face Harmond. "Look, we don't have time for this. If they land, it is, as you say, game over for us all unless I stop them."

"How do I know it is not the other way around?"

Erin ran though the portal and stopped alongside Jack. All

guns shifted, pointing at Erin. Jack's eyes went wide. "Erin! What are you doing?"

Erin glared at him, then all the men and their weapons. "Look, he is right, we don't have time for this. If he was here to harm you, he could have already. You need to trust him."

Harmond's eyes narrowed. "Lady, I don't know who you are, or him for that matter. And if I don't believe him, why should I believe you?"

Erin rolled her eyes. "You don't need to trust me or him. Trust your instincts. Why would he even come out here and talk to you when he could have just lifted off and you would have been none the wiser?"

"Because his computer said *now*, he could lift off."

Erin smiled. "And who is to say he couldn't before and the computer is reminding? After all it is his ship right?"

Harmond waved his hands lower and all the weapons followed suit. "You have a point."

"Sir, we need to lift off in the next few points if we are to meet them before they can get too close to stop them in orbit," Kan's voice echoed from the open corridor.

Jack turned and stepped one foot inside the open portal, then looked back. "Harmond, get your people out of here. If we lift off with you this close, it won't be pretty."

Harmond nodded. "Right. Men move back, out of the clearing." Monroe sat hunched over his computer with the dish pointed at the open portal desperately trying to get it working again. Harmond pulled him to his feet. "That goes for you too."

"But Sir, I might be able to–"

Harmond shook his head. "Doesn't matter, I am not losing a man because he had a stupid moment. Now GO!"

Monroe picked up his laptop and the antenna. "Yes Sir." He ran after the other men.

Harmond waved to Jack. "Good luck, I have a strange hunch you are going to need it."

Jack stepped inside the rest of the way. "Thanks. You don't know the half of it." He spun around and held up his hand blocking Erin. "No, you stay here."

Erin blinked. "Are you nuts? Do you think I am going to leave you now?"

"Yes you are. You know what I am planning."

"You darn right I do! And if you think you can leave me here, you got another thing coming." She dove though the portal before Jack could close it.

Jack blinked several times looking at the woman at his feet. "Erin! You can't–"

"You need to learn when you have lost an argument, and you have lost this one," she said standing up.

Jack closed his eyes and sighed. "All right. Kan, lift off."

Kan's screen appeared from the wall. "Acknowledged. Main drives are online. Inertia systems activated. Lifting off." They felt a slight vibration through the floor as the powerful drives fired up and pushed them into the sky. "We will approach the target in two minutes."

Jack grabbed Erin, and they ran for the control room. The seats had already reformed and were ready for them. They sat as the chairs added extra padding and pulled them closer to the controls.

Erin squeezed Jack's hand not letting go. "Thank you for letting me stay."

Jack cracked a grin. "Like I had a choice." He checked several of the readouts being displayed on the screens. "Kan, can you give us a visual on the other ship?"

Kan's screen emerged from the wall and flashed. "Yes, one moment." The top screen cleared and showed nothing for a few seconds, then the sleek, contoured lines gave an almost organic nature to the Kryllin jump ship appeared as the invisibility screen was lowered. "Now being displayed on the main screen. They have detected us, slowed their approach, and are trying to initiate communications. Shall I do the same and establish a connection?"

Jack sighed as he glanced towards Erin. "I know they won't listen but I have to try. Yes, and keep Erin out of the image. Also, drop the invisibility screen."

"Understood. Connection established."

The screen changed and displayed a lanky man with several arms. His head was elongated compared to a normal human. His large eyebrow rose. "I am Da'Kon of the Kryllin. Who is this? You are not Ra'Toth."

"No, I am K'lan."

"K'lan? What are you doing in Ra'Toth's ship? Where is Ra'Toth?"

"There was an incident. The containment of the gravity drive aboard my ship collapsed. Ra'Toth was inside at the time."

"I see. Do you have data on this very unusual 'incident'?"

"I will transmit it later. I have an alpha red imperative. The mission here is a failure. What we hoped to find is not here. Our energies must be focused elsewhere immediately."

Da'Kon's long narrow eyebrow scrunched up. "You know I cannot accept an alpha red imperative without the proper authorization. Only the council can authorize that, and they haven't."

"Are you sure?"

Da'Kon's engineer spoke up. "Sir, it is possible that

there has been an alpha red. This ship's long range communications are very basic and under powered to help with the stability of the jump drive."

Da'Kon turned. "Can we verify what he says is true?"

The engineer nodded. "Yes, it will take time. And we will need to divert most of the power available to boost the weak signal."

"Do it!" Da'Kon turned back to the screen and faced Jack. "We have to verify this. Please stand by." The image winked out.

Erin squeezed Jack's hand again. "Now what?"

Jack sighed. "Now we do the only thing we can. Kan, ready the drives. Engage full speed ahead."

Erin blinked. "But–"

"We can't let them contact the homeworld. If they are cut off in mid communication, another ship will follow. If we can take them out beforehand, the council won't take the risk."

Erin rolled her eyes. "You hope."

"We all hope. Kan, aim for one of the cylindrical protrusions on the center of the hull. They should be part of the jump drive."

Kan's screen flashed. "Full power to drives. Impact in 10 micro-points."

Looking around the room that was about to become her tomb, it occurred to her the shape was a bit different from Jack's ship. She tried to put her finger on why. The deep lines and ridges that went from the floor to the ceiling compared to Jack's perfectly smooth walls. The ridges seemed to be groves outside the wall, almost if the bulkheads were doubled and yet ...Something tugged at her subconscious. Where had she seen something like this before? Kan's screen flashed. "Impact in five micro-points."

Erin's eyes went wide. "Kan! Emergency eject of this room!"

Kan's screen flashed. "Control room decoupling system found and online … activating. Brace yourselves, inertia control system will be offline."

Jack whipped his head to the right and eyed Erin. "Control room ejec–"

They were slammed into their seats as latches around the circular control room decoupled from the ship and a large engine below them fired.

Da'Kon blinked. "What in the homeworld are they doing? They are going to hit. Get K'lan on the screen now!"

"He is not responding."

"Get us out of here!"

"I can't! The drives were rerouted into the communication array. It will take me at least three points to switch back." The engineer's multiple tendrils moved so fast they were a blur as he readjusted the power feeds.

"No time!" the navigator said as the ships collided. The spear headed point of Ra'Toth's ship struck one of the cylindrical extensions and dove into the superstructure, crumpling and buckling the hull as it went. A second before impact a disc shaped section of the top decoupled and slid away from Ra'Toth's ship. Both ships were sent careening from the impact. Now joined at the hip, they spun faster and faster.

Alarms blared as several side consoles exploded and acrid smoke poured from them. Da'Kon and his crew fought not to be thrown from their chairs. Lights flickered. "Status report!"

"The main core has been breached and we are looking at a containment failure of the jump drive in two points."

"Anyway to shut down the drive?"

"Negative, we sustained a direct hit in one of the jump manifolds."

"Decouple the drive section and leave it. The emergency system should be able to get us planet side where we can contact the council."

The engineer shook his head. "The system was damaged from the impact."

The ship began to spin faster than ever before. Da'Kon spat. "This ship isn't worth a teldar's turd!"

Several more consoles exploded before sending ripples throughout the systems. The navigator was tossed backwards, his face blackened from his console erupting. There was a bright flash as containment was lost and the ship glowed with jump energy, brighter and brighter. Then another flash at the center and everything began to fall in upon itself, imploding. Panels fell off and flipped towards the center, the superstructures buckled then twisted like spaghetti before being sucked into the gravity well. As if a bomb happened in reverse. Then a final flash and there was no trace of either ship.

Jack looked out at the stars through the transparent hull and sighed. "Kan, did they manage to send anything to the council?"

"Negative. While I did detect a few weak signals at the last moment, they will never reach the homeworld."

Jack gazed over at Erin and smiled. "How did you know about the control room eject system? Heck, even I never knew any of our ships had it."

"I saw how Ra'Toth's control room was different, and it reminded me of an escape pod in an old movie." She shrugged. "I thought it couldn't hurt to try." She smiled and squeezed his hand again. "And you wanted to leave me behind."

Jack rolled his eyes. "I get the feeling that I am never going to live that down. And Kan, why didn't YOU tell me about the eject system?"

Kan's screen flashed. "Until that moment, I did not know about it. Once Erin gave the command, I checked, and she was right. I am sorry Sir, but Ra'Toth's ship was very different from ours in several respects. I am still processing some of the data in the core."

Jack blinked. "Core? What core? We left it behind."

"The main data core yes, but this control room also has a backup data core and power systems. They are smaller, but adequate."

Jack felt a bump as the ejected room shook. "Kan? What was that?"

"I am sorry Sir, the engines in this detached room are not as strong as I would like. The inertia of the ejection and the extra burn to get us to a minimum safe distance in time has added to the gravitational pull of the planet. I am unable to stop our decent given the time allotted."

Erin's face went white. "Are we going to burn up?"

Kan's screen flickered. "Negative. While the engines are not strong enough to counteract the gravitational pull of the planet in time, I can control our decent. We will land at or near the site of our original ship."

The small room shook even more as the lights and screens went dark. "Kan? How sure are you about this landing?" Jack said looking at the Earth getting larger by the second.

No response.

"Kan?"

"Sorry Sir, I am here. It is proving to be more difficult than I originally estimated."

Erin gripped the chair. "What happened to the lights and screens?"

"I have reduced power consumption as much as possible to reinforce the shields and engines. I am afraid it is going to be a bumpy ride."

Jack's eyes narrowed. "Kan, you don't have emotions."

"Sir, at this moment, I can wholeheartedly say I DO. Hold on, correction thrust firing." They felt a jolt to the right as their course corrected. But then the room started to spin.

"Kan! What is going on?" Erin said as she snapped her eyes shut.

"I am sorry, this is proving to be far more difficult without proper engines. Firing a counter spin." The room slowed and stopped its spin, but it also threw them off course. "Firing another correction."

For every correction, Kan had to do a counter correction. It became a dance of spin and stop, then spin again. Erin held onto her stomach as the room shook harder and flames licked the outside.

Erin wiped the sweat from her forehead. "It's getting warm in here."

"Kan, we need more cooling," Jack said.

Kan's screen flickered dimly. "I am sorry Sir, there is not adequate power for that. But I do not think the heat will rise above Erin's tolerance."

Erin blinked. "It already is!"

"I should have been more specific, it should not prove fatal."

Erin rolled her eyes as she pulled back her sweat soaked

hair. The chair, not designed for human sweat, became sticky. "Great, love the confidence there."

Jack looked over at Erin. The light of the inferno outside lit her in a flickering orange glow. He could see how hot she was. And the chair couldn't be helping. It was not designed for humans and had to be exacerbating the problem, trapping the heat next to her rather than carrying it away as it should. If they had the power, it could have modified itself. Another engine burn threw them into a spin. "Kan, status?"

"Progressing, landing in fifteen points. Course may be erratic, but it is also reducing our speed. Landing site is still the same."

Jack squeezed Erin's very warm hand. "I don't think Erin will last in this heat for that long. Are you sure you can't increase the cooling systems? Even if we pick another landing site?"

Kan's dim screen flickered. "Negative. It is taking all available power to maintain control. I cannot increasing the cooling systems without sacrificing control. I am sorry Sir."

Erin wheezed. "Don't worry about me, you aren't getting rid of me that easy."

"But I do. You are going to boil in your own skin." Jack's eyes flashed. "I have an idea. Just relax, this may feel weird."

Erin blinked as she turned her head. "What will?" Jack liquified and flowed over Erin covering every part but her face, then he slipped under her clothing touching her skin directly. It felt as if he was in constant motion all over her body. "Jack? What are you doing? It feels like you are massaging every inch of me." Her eyes went wide as she gasped. "JACK! Not there! Not now!"

"Sorry, I am trying to cool you. I can regulate my temperature and yours by flowing around at a–."

Her eyes rolled back. "Not there! You don't need to ...oh my God ...STOP! Not there!"

"But you need cooling there as well."

"Jack!" she screamed.

"Okay, I will try to not flow around there so much. And here I thought you'd like it."

"I would, if we weren't plunging into the Earth and may burn up. This is not the time to send me into screaming orgasms!"

"Well, it would keep your mind off of the–."

"Jack!"

"I won't. But I do admit it is tempting." They felt another jolt as strong engine burn went off. "Kan?"

"Sorry Sir, couldn't be helped. But I have managed to slow our decent further and we are back on course. Landing in five points."

Erin looked out and saw while the flames had reduced. "That should help with the heat in here, right?"

Kan's dim display flashed. "Correct. I have detected some change in the ambient internal temperature."

Sweat dripped off of Erin's brow. "Wouldn't know it by me. It's still hotter in here than the Sahara and Death Valley put together."

"Final landing in two units, brace yourselves it is going to be rough. But I am certain the shields will hold. Although, we may leave a large scar on the planet's surface."

"Kan, Erin won't survive such a sudden impact. Transfer all power to engines and slow us down as much as possible."

"But Sir, if I do that the damage to this vessel will be extreme. The power sources may regenerate, but the engines will be damaged beyond conventional repair."

"I understand, do it."

Kan's screen flickered. "Acknowledged. Dropping shields and transferring all remaining power to engines."

They felt a strong increase in gravity as the engines fired.

Erin gulped. "Jack! I am getting heavy."

"I know, can't be helped. Hold on, just a few more minutes."

They looked out and saw what resembled green grass a few moments earlier, were in fact trees. And they were still hurtling towards them. Kan tilted the room and fired the engines in another powerful burn, reducing the speed even further. The rushing of land slowed from a blur to a few trees passing by the window as one might see while driving a car.

"Landing in 5 ... 4 ... brace yourselves ... "

"Erin, hold your breath." Erin sucked in a deep breath and Jack covered her face and changed his shape into a large ball surrounding the chair.

Kan's screen flashed. "3 ... 2 ... 1." There was a mighty crack as the room impacted the ground. The engines crumpled as if they were tinfoil. The super structure, stronger and lighter than anything man had made bowed and waved before the whole thing split in two absorbing the impact.

Jack flowed off of Erin and she gasped. "Kan? Status?"

No response.

Erin coughed as she sat up and tried to stand, only to fall back into the chair. "Kan?"

The small portable screen on the console flickered, then glowed brighter. "I am here. This vessel is severely damaged, engines are damaged beyond repair, as are the shield generators. All power systems are offline."

Erin blinked as she managed to stand. "Then how are you talking to us?"

"My portable system still has power."

Jack reformed into his human shape, added clothes, and looked around. "We had better get out of here. No doubt we were seen coming down." He walked over and tried to disconnected Kan from the control console, but couldn't. Nor could he move him. "Kan? I can't remove you from the console."

"Sorry Sir, I had to bond to the console to prevent me from being thrown around the room during reentry. One moment." The surface of the console glowed for a second, then subsided. "You should now be able to remove me."

Jack pulled at the cable, and it disconnected with ease. He picked up Kan. "There we go."

"Sir, please remove the alternate data core as well. It is located behind the lower panel, to the right of your position."

"Why? I am sure it is junk like the rest."

Kan's screen flickered. "The unit itself should have survived. And it may contain data that we might find useful. However, I will not be able to access it until I am whole again. I do not have enough energy to power it up at this point in time."

Jack set Kan down, took two steps over and slid back a panel revealing a twelve inch black cube with several organic looking connections radiating out. He carefully removed each one and slid out the cube. "Well it does look to be intact." He placed it in the backpack, slipped it on his shoulder, picked up Kan, took Erin's hand, and smiled. Let's get out of here."

Erin blinked. "Are we going to leave this?"

"Well I can't stick it in my pocket. What do you want me to do?"

"I just think it would be better the less we leave behind."

Jack shrugged. "I agree, but there is nothing I can do."

The small screen flickered in Jack's hand. "I have a suggestion. If you plug me back into the console, I can activate a nano-dissolve.

Jack glared at the screen. "Are you kidding? It has that?"

"Yes, it will take most of my reserve power, but I can recharge once I am reunited with my full core."

Jack shook his head. "Unbelievable. I didn't give Ra'Toth enough credit."

Erin blinked. "What? What does it have?"

"A nano-disslove. We developed the technology to allow the atoms in an object disconnect and fall apart into their basic elements. Not many ships had the ability added to their makeup though as we always had the option to collapse the gravity drive. And it is cleaner. This will leave a pile of dust behind, but I suspect whoever finds it will assume it was burned up in reentry and only the dust remained." Jack plugged Kan into the console and it lit up.

Kan's screen dimmed and flickered. "It is activated. Sixty micro-points until dissolution."

Jack unplugged Kan, grabbed Erin's hand again, and smiled. "We are outta here."

They ran out what was left of Ra'Toth's ship and turned around in time to see it dissolve to black and white dust.

Erin whistled. "Wow."

Jack smiled. "Pretty amazing isn't it. This is the first time I have seen it used."

Kan's screen flickered. "It was successful, no one will know what happened. Shutting down to conserve energy." His screen went black.

Harmond and his men were halfway back to their vehicles when a call came through on the satellite radio. Monroe pulled the radio from his pack and answered it. "Yes Sir, he is here. One moment." He handed the bulky handheld device to Harmond. "It's General Compton, Sir."

Harmond raised the device to his ear. "Harmond here, is there a problem General?"

There was a grunt sound on the other end. "I see by the cryptic report you left, that your team is out investigating something energy related?"

Harmond stiffened. "Yes Sir, is that a problem?"

"Yes, I want those under my command to file more information than *that* when they head out in the field. But we will discuss it later. I see you are in a forest heading towards your vehicles. I assume you are returning?"

"Yes Sir, our experiments are concluded."

"Good, then you won't mind checking out an unusual situation on your way."

Harmond gulped. "Unusual situation?"

"Yes, we detected a large unidentified object that appeared in orbit. Then another larger object appeared, they collided, and something much smaller crashed not far from your position."

Harmond's eyes went wide as he leaned into the handset. "Something came back down?"

"Yes, very unusual wouldn't you say? It appears to be in a clearing north east of your position."

"Yes Sir, very much. And I know the clearing, we were there earlier today."

"Is that so? Anything you would care to inform me about?"

Harmond gulped again. "Not at this time, Sir."

"I thought as much. We will discuss this situation in full when you get back here. In the mean time check out that landing site. If you find anything I want to be informed ASAP, is that understood? But do not give details over this link. I will join you."

Harmond gulped a third time. "You will Sir?"

"You had better believe it. Compton . . . out."

Harmond gave the handset back to Monroe. "We have new orders, we are to go back to that first clearing and see if anything survived a landing."

Monroe cocked an eyebrow. "They came back down, sir?"

"Yes, or a piece of them did. The general said it was a smaller piece of the larger object."

"So they were seen."

"Somewhat, I don't have all the details. But General Compton didn't say they took off, but rather suddenly appeared in orbit. A collision between them and another object were detected, that's all. All right men, head northeast back to that clearing. Double-time! I would like to get back to the base before nightfall."

"Yes Sir!" the men said in unison.

Several hours later they reached the clearing. The earth

showed a large blackened skid mark several meters long, and at the end a pile of white and black ash. Nothing else.

Monroe sighed. "Looks like they burned up on reentry."

Harmond shook his head. "With their technology, I very much doubt that."

"Sir!" one of the men shouted and waved his hand. "I think I may have something."

Harmond ran over. "What did you find?"

"This." The man pointed to a faint boot print in the grass. "I only found one, but it is the same size and type we found in the other location."

"So they did survive."

"But Sir, if they did, there should be some signs of a ship here. All we see is dust."

Harmond glanced over towards the carved swath and the colored dust at the end. "If a people have the technology to hide their ship from our view, then it is quite possible they could also have it fall to dust if needed."

Monroe cocked his head as he walked over to the dust pile. "I suppose that is possible Sir. Upon closer inspection, this does not look like normal dust to me."

Harmond nodded. "Yes, exactly. Men document the area and contain that dust before a good wind scatters it. Although, I suspect a lot of it is missing by now."

Monroe held up his hand. "Sir, how do you expect us to do that? We didn't bring a bunch of containers with us."

"Then cover up the rest with your emergency Mylar blankets! I will not have General Compton telling me I failed to secure the area. Understood?"

The men nodded. "Yes Sir."

"Good, and give me that radio, I need to talk with the general."

"Yes Sir," Monroe said as he handed over the handset.

Harmond adjusted the frequency and hit the transmit button. "General Compton, this is Colonel Harmond. Do you receive me?"

Compton's voice came through the handset loud and clear. "I do colonel, what is the status?"

"We have an interesting situation here, Sir."

"Is it what we expected?"

"Not exactly, but something very interesting. I assume you will be here soon?"

"I will. Secure the area."

Harmond glanced around. His men were patrolling the area, and the dust was covered by shiny silver blankets. "Already done."

"Good. Compton . . . out."

Harmond handed the handset back to Monroe. "What did he say sir?"

"He will be here soon, and we are to secure the area."

"Which we have done."

"Now we have to keep it that way."

Several hours later General Compton appeared with three teams of men carrying equipment. His wispy white hair may have showed his age, but his body displayed a fit, muscular man ready to join his men wherever they may be. Harmond saluted. "Welcome General, I didn't expect you to arrive so soon."

General Compton gestured to a rise in the distance. "We were able to get to that ridge before needing to proceed on foot. Status?"

"We have secured the area as instructed. But this is what I wanted to show you." Harmond walked over to the area covered by shiny Mylar and pulled it back. "As you can see something hit the dirt with surprising force and heat. But nothing remains of whatever it was."

Compton's eyes narrowed. "Other than this white and black dust?"

Harmond nodded. "Yes Sir."

Compton turned to Harmond as his eyes narrowed further. "Now, was there anything you wanted to tell me?"

"Well, Sir, there were other developments that proceeded our field mission."

"Which are? Your report was more cryptic than a cryptographers key."

Harmond stiffened. "We detected an unusual high intensity energy signature. When it reappeared a second time, we were able to determine its location. Because of its unusual nature, I thought it might be a system glitch, and I did not want to bother you until I had something more concrete."

Compton nodded. "I see. You made the right decision. Now were there any other developments since then?"

"Yes Sir, there was. We first came here and didn't find anything other than a small black hole in the ground. Then we detected another signature. We found the source."

"Which was?"

"A craft of some sort. Hard to say as it was invisible."

"What! And you didn't detain it or those inside?"

Harmond stiffened further. "No Sir. The occupants came out and informed me of a hostile ship in orbit and the only chance to stop them was to let the those in front of me take off."

Compton raised his hands over his head. "And you believed them?"

"Not at first Sir, but then they made a good argument. If

their race could hide an entire ship from view, they could have eliminated us without blinking an eye."

"So, they had eyes?"

"Yes Sir, they looked human. One male, one female."

"But still, if true, they could have taken off without talking to you."

"That is true Sir. But they didn't wish to harm us."

The general blinked. "How do you figure that?"

"They said if we were close to the ship when it lifted off, it would have been deadly. Considering that they did not have to come out at all, then it would seem they were telling the truth. And your monitoring of the objects in orbit would further confirm what they said."

The general turned away put his hands behind his back, took several steps, then turned around, and walked back. "You did the right thing based on all the information at hand. While we don't have all the facts, it would appear they did not wish to harm us while someone else did." He looked over at the black and white dust then turned back to Harmond while his eyes narrowed. "This whole incident is to be kept internal. While I agree they didn't mean us any harm, there are other branches that will take a different approach. Is that understood?"

Harmond nodded. "Perfectly Sir. And I agree."

"Good. Now bag this stuff up and get it back to the base. Perhaps we can learn something from it. If not, at least we tried. It is a shame they had to perish after helping us."

Harmond rose a finger. "I don't think they did."

General Compton tilted his head. "What do you mean? How could they have survived this?"

"I suspect they did, but then destroyed what was left to hide evidence. You said yourself that what came down was much smaller than the original object. A life boat of some sort."

Compton nodded. "Makes sense. See if you can find them, but do it quietly. If we can keep it off the record, they may answer our questions."

"Understood Sir." Harmond raised his voice. "All right men, catalog the area, bag this dust up, and return to base." He his eyes focused back on the general. "Will you be staying sir?"

"No. I will return to base, I know you have the situation well in hand."

Harmond saluted. "Thank you Sir."

Compton returned the salute. "Carry on." He turned and with two other men made his way back to the ridge, and his vehicle.

— 18 —

Erin awoke and reached over to find Jack missing. It was still dark. She sat up quick and grumbled. They had a wonderful time of intimate celebration after getting back home, but to find him gone …again. She got up, pulled on her clothes and went downstairs. No sign of him. Then her eyes flashed, and she went down to the basement. Sure enough, inside the hidden area, she found Jack.

Kan's console screen flashed. "Sir, if you connect that last data line, I should be able to access the core from Ra'Toth's control room."

Jack connected something that resembled a small snake to the top of the core. "Done. Try it now." Several of the lines glowed and wiggled slightly as they configured themselves. The core glowed with energy.

"I have access. Some data is damaged, but I should be able to reconstitute it from the fragments."

Erin leaned on the brick wall. "So what are you two up to now?"

Jack whirled around. "Erin! I thought you were sleeping?"

"I was, until you left. Don't you know when you leave a wife like that, they feel it, and wake up?"

Jack sighed. "Well I thought if I was quiet enough you

wouldn't notice."

"With some women yes, but not me, not now. I will always notice. Now I ask again, what are you two up to?"

Kan's screen flickered. "We are attempting to access the core from Ra'Toth's ship. While successful, there is damage to the data and I am attempting to reconstitute it."

"How long until that is completed?"

"At least several units."

"Several hours then? Good." She grabbed Jack's hand. "Come on back up to bed with your wife."

"But I am not tired, and I can continue working."

"You may not be, but I am. And I sleep better with you, than without."

Kan's screen flashed. "Sir, most of my abilities are working on the core. Therefore, there is little you can do at the moment."

"There. See? You can't do anything here anyway."

Jack smiled. "All right my darling. Lead the way."

Erin led him upstairs, and they lay upon the bed. A few minutes later she fell asleep wrapped in Jack's strong arms. Hours later light streamed into the window waking her. She smiled seeing herself still being held by Jack. She turned to see his smiling face.

"I was wondering when you were going to wake up."

She squeezed his arm. "It is good to see you when I wake."

"Then I shall make sure it happens more often." He kissed her lips and her heart jumped. He pulled away and sighed. "But now I need to see how Kan made out with that core."

Erin sighed and peeled herself away. "I will go make breakfast then."

A little while later she poked her nose inside the hidden room. "Jack? I called a while ago. Your eggs are getting cold."

Jack sat hunched over a console. One of his arms ended in a liquid pool on the control surface. "In a minute."

"You said that five minutes ago."

"Sorry but Kan has found something very interesting."

"Has he finished rebuilding the core?"

Kan's screen flashed. "Negative. However, it is 95% complete."

Erin leaned over Jack's shoulder. "What did he find?"

"More results data from Ra'Toth's testing. Also, some old data with speculation on where in our genome the deterioration is centered. We have long suspected it had to do with our longevity changes, but this goes into much more detail."

Jack sat back and the red blob at the end of his arm reformed into a hand. "It is interesting that was left out of the data we downloaded from the council's systems."

Kan's screen flashed. "It may have been something the council determined inaccurate, but Ra'Toth thought otherwise."

Jack looked off then back again. "While that might be true, knowing how close Ra'Toth was with the council, it is very unlikely. I tend to think this information is very significant."

Erin pointed at the data scrolling past. "It is possible that Ra'Toth found it and never told the council?"

"I suppose it is possible he thought it would diminish his status," Jack said rubbing his chin. "It is so old, many would wonder about its reliability."

Erin turned, and she stared at Jack. "Are you telling me that with all of your technology, you still have problems with information being lost?"

Jack sighed. "Yes. It is hard to keep track of everything. The network is very robust, but accidents can occur. And if someone thought it might hurt their status in the long run, for whatever reason, they may try to rewrite or delete information that was problematic."

Erin shook her head. "Political problems exist everywhere in the universe."

Jack shrugged. "So it would appear. Not to mention any information like this, that reemerges after being missing for so long, is scrutinized and suspected to be a ploy to forward their status." Jack turned in his chair. "And they may never be able to prove its authenticity. If they can't with absolute certainty, then it will harm, rather than help them. Because of the previous instances, it is rare for a Kryllin to try. Even if they know the information to be true."

"And if it means the survival of your race?"

"Up till now, we always thought we had time on our side. And most of my people still do."

Erin sat in Jack's lap and he wrapped his strong arms around her. She put her head in the crux of Jack's neck. "And Ra'Toth?"

"Whatever Ra'Toth knew, I am sure so did the council. Although I can't prove it, I would like to know everything he did. It might prove useful in finding a cure, or at the very least, keep the council off of our backs."

Erin sat up. "I thought you said they wouldn't show up after we destroyed the ship?"

Jack's lip curled. "I said they shouldn't bother us. But if they get desperate enough, they may assume that Ra'Toth was on to something and try again. I doubt it will happen."

"If you don't think it will happen, then why all of this?" Erin pointed to the core, and the console connected to it.

"I don't. But I like to, as you say, hedge my bets."

The doorbell rang.

Erin blinked. "Are you expecting anyone?"

Jack shook his head. "No, are you?"

"Nope. Probably Jane. I did tell her I would call, and it has been over a day."

"Well you had better go talk with her then," Jack winked.

Erin slid out of Jack's lap, stood up, and made her way out of the basement to the front door. But when she opened it, her eyes went wide.

Colonel Harmond stood there in his dress blue uniform, his cover held firmly under his arm. He smiled as he spoke. "Hello, Mrs. Winecker, we meet again."

"What … how … who …"

Harmond's smile broadened. "I don't think we were properly introduced earlier. I am Colonel Harmond. Is your husband around?"

Erin sputtered. "Jack? No, he … he is …"

"Mrs. Winecker, there is no need for deception. I can tell from the look on your face he is here. I assure you I mean him no harm, nor you. Look around. I came alone."

Erin peered past Harmond, saw his car, but didn't see anyone else. "But your men could be hidden."

Harmond nodded keeping the smile in place. "They could be, but they aren't."

Jack raced up the stairs. "Erin! I think I found …" He stopped dead when he saw the man in uniform at the door.

Harmond smiled at Jack. "Please, don't stop on my account Mr. Winecker."

Jack walked over to Erin. "He knows our names?" he said out of the corner of his mouth.

"Yes I do. And I have excellent hearing. Beyond normal range I assure you. Now if you would like I can come in, or we can talk out here. Either is fine with me."

"Come in then," Jack said.

"Jack!" Erin blurted out.

"If he wanted to storm the house, he would have by now. He trusted us, I feel we owe him the same."

Harmond nodded as he entered. "Thank You."

Erin gestured to the chair in the living room and Harmond sat down. Erin and Jack sat down opposite him on the couch. "How did you find us?"

"Facial recognition."

Jack's eyebrows went up. "But your equipment was not functional by the time I exited the ship."

Harmond laughed. "I figured you knew that. But what you didn't know is I have a photographic memory. Based on that and with the help of some software I was able to create a composite close enough to match Jack Winecker's military records. Or should I say the original Jack Winecker, as I am certain you are not him."

Jack sat back on the couch. "Very perceptive."

"Thank you. I also suspect that Erin here is the original, otherwise the display back at the clearing would have been very different."

Erin looked back and forth but didn't say anything. After a minute, Jack spoke. "Again, perceptive. My question is, what do you plan to do with this information?"

Harmond sat back in his chair for the first time. "Nothing."

Jack and Erin blinked. "Nothing?" they said in unison.

"That's right. Nothing. And my commanding officer General Compton agrees with me."

"But what about–"

"Someone else? Not going to happen. General Compton has sealed or destroyed everything regarding this incident. Everyone has been sworn to secrecy, and they know what would happen if they were to break it. We all know you acted on our behalf, that is clear even if we don't know the details."

Jack gazed out the window then back. "We are dying. My people wanted to use humans in experiments to try to find a solution. I had to stop them. Even if it means the end of my race."

"I see, and what makes you think they won't try again?"

"That explanation is very detailed and political in nature. But in summary, the council will not want to pursue this option as it has cost them too much at this point."

Harmond nodded as he turned his cover in his hand. "That I can understand. However, I would like to request that you be available should your assessment of the situation be in error."

Jack studied Harmond and his eyes narrowed. "You mean help you fight them?"

"If it came to that."

Jack laughed. "I don't think you understand how much more advanced they are. They could come to this planet, do what they wanted, and you would never see it coming. Why do you think I took matters into my own hands?"

"Yes I assumed as much. But it is more in line of asking you to help again with the technology at your disposal. I am sure you have another ship that could be used."

"I do have equipment yes. But as I said, you will never see them coming."

Harmond stood and put his cover back on his head. "Yes, and this is why we want you to keep in touch. Without you, we have no hope."

Jack stood. "That's right you don't. So I suggest you leave me and my wife alone."

Harmond smiled. "I think you misunderstand, that has

been done. I am asking for your help again, in the future, should it be needed."

"And you shall have it." Jack walked towards the door with Erin in tow and opened it.

Harmond started walking towards the door. "That is all I ask." He stepped through then turned. "And on behalf of Earth, we thank you." He bowed slightly and headed towards the waiting car.

19

After they saw Harmond drive away, Erin turned to Jack. "Now what did you find?"

"Hmm? Ohh! Yes, Kan has found something very unusual. Come take a look." He grabbed her hand and led her down to the basement.

Inside the hidden room, Kan's screen flashed as a green beam reached out and touched everything in the room then retracted. "I have finished recovering the data in the core."

Jack sat down. "Good. What did you find?"

Upstairs the front door cracked, splintered and fell in. "K'lan! I know you are here! Face me, you traitor!"

Down below Jack and Erin's eyes went wide at the sound of Ra'Toth's voice. Jack mouthed to Erin. "Stay here!"

Jack stepped outside the workroom and sealed it. He then liquified himself, entered an old vent, raced up upward, and emerged to reform behind Ra'Toth who had entered the living room. "I am here Ra'Toth."

Ra'Toth spun around. "There you are! You traitor! When I get through with you there won't be enough atoms left to identify your signature."

Jack took a step back towards the open doorway. "How did you survive?"

"You would like to know wouldn't you? You should have known it is almost impossible to kill a Kryllin of my age."

"So I have heard. Apparently, even a gravity well can't."

"It can. And it came very close."

Jack took another step back. "Then how did you–"

"Survive? I broke out of that prison you put me in a few micro-points before the drive went critical. Then it was a simple matter of getting away."

"Simple? It couldn't have been simple. I was farther away from the drive and I was almost engulfed by it."

Ra'Toth allowed a grin to crack his lips. "It was to me. I reformed into a double sided drill and went through the floor as it was cracking. I entered the soil and kept going. Sealing the hole behind me with dirt as I went. By that time the pull increased beyond my tolerance, I was out of range."

"But we didn't see any sign that the dirt was disturbed."

Ra'Toth laughed. "Ah but you did. The small black hole in the dirt? That wasn't only the drive's doing."

"That is where you drilled?"

Ra'Toth nodded. "Yes, I was almost pulled into the gravity well before I started drilling. Hence, I left no trace. But enough of this!" Ra'Toth lashed out with an arm that shifted into a tendril that grabbed Jack around the neck. Jack liquified and slid from his grasp then rolled for the doorway. Ra'Toth lashed out again with a diamond hard point but hit the grandfather clock instead. The glass shattered and the wood split in half. A loud CHANG went off as the chimes hit each other. "I taught you well." Ra'Toth liquified then rolled after Jack.

Down in the basement Erin tried to open the door. "What is wrong with this thing?" She banged on the open control switch.

Kan's screen flashed. "That won't help. I have sealed this room."

Erin spun around. "What? Why?"

"To prevent Ra'Toth from finding us."

Erin glared and stomped her foot. "Kan! You open this door right now!"

"I will not."

"But Jack is out there!"

"I am well aware of that. But I am following his instructions."

"Blast his instructions. You open this door right now or I will pull out every wire you have!"

Erin swore she heard a gulp then Kan's screen flashed but very dimly. "If you will listen, there is a plan. And I will need your assistance."

Erin glared and started walking towards Kan's console. "Talk and fast. And if I don't like what I am hearing, I'm going to start tearing you apart!"

Kan's screen flashed fast. "Erin, if you notice the fabricator has been working all this time. If you will help me, we can assemble a device that will help K'lan."

Erin stopped. "And what is going to help Jack? He told me Ra'Toth is much stronger."

"That is correct, but if you finish building the device I am fabricating. It will stop him."

"A weapon?"

Kan's screen flashed a little slower. "Yes. I have most of the components completed. Only one left. It should be done in fifteen micro-points." Erin heard a soft beep, and the glow went out from the circular base of the fabricator as it shut down. "It is done. Now if you will follow my instructions, you can build the device."

Jack reformed and dove as Ra'Toth's diamond tipped tendril plowed into a tree splitting it in two. Ra'Toth shot out with another tendril to block Jack, but he narrowed his body just in time. He reformed into a wheel and rolled out of range. "Hold still and take your punishment like a Kryllin!"

"Sorry, no," Jack said as he kept rolling.

Ra'Toth took after him. "I taught you too well. But I didn't teach you all!" Ra'Toth dove to the ground and flattened himself into a plain and shot forward covering the grass with incredible speed. He got under Jack as he was rolling away and flipped him high into the air. Ra'Toth reformed and shot a tendril up after Jack. But at the last second Jack's wheel shape formed wings and glided out of his reach. "Nice trick. One I didn't teach you."

Jack reformed his center into a rough human shape, flew into an air current, and went higher. Ra'Toth glared. "You can't get away that easy!" He liquified and shot up like a compressed rubber ball. High in the air he reformed into a human shape with wings, then his lower torso changed into a large tail with a laser sharp point.

Jack looked back to see Ra'Toth right behind. He dove but not in time to avoid the impact. The tail sliced deep into his leg and threw off his concentration. He hit the ground hard, plowing up dirt as he went. Jack stood up and shook. His leg had a deep wound, and it refused to seal itself. He limped two steps before Ra'Toth reformed the tail into legs and landed.

"Having trouble with your leg?" Ra'Toth sneered.

"What did you do?"

Ra'Toth's arms became tendrils with spear points at the end. "A little trick I learned long ago, and never told you about. You can temporally disrupt the shifting of another Kryllin if you know their signature. And I do know yours."

"And I know yours!"

Ra'Toth nodded. "Yes you do. But you don't know how to use the information, while I on the other hand ... " Ra'Toth lashed out with one of the tendrils, but Jack moved in the last second. He missed Jack's arm by inches. "Dang it! Hold still! It will be much easier for you in the end."

"Never!" Jack reformed into a wheel with a leg sticking out to the side and rolled away.

Ra'Toth lashed out again with a tendril and dug into the dirt in front of Jack, he rolled into it and another tendril grabbed him. Ra'Toth's form shrank down to more human size as he grinned. Several more tendrils split from the other two, all ending in sharp points surrounding and poised to dig into Jack. "Any last words?"

Jack struggled but to no avail. Ra'Toth was too strong. "You said it was only temporary!"

"It is. But enough of them will disrupt your signature and your cells will lose cohesion. Something else not many Kryllin's know."

"Let him go!" Erin shouted.

Ra'Toth turned to see Erin standing on the porch pointing a weapon at him. "Well well well, what have we here? The little female pointing a weapon at me. I would kill you where you stand, if it wasn't so amusing. Your weapons are so far behind ours, the most it could do is make me blink. And even that is questionable."

Erin's look didn't change and her finger tightened on the trigger. "Look closer. I dare you."

Ra'Toth's eyes narrowed as he noticed the sleek barrel, the tightly hidden energy core in the grip, and the tiny scope with its wall piercing enhanced vision. His eyes went wide as Erin grinned. "That's right. It is Kryllin. Now let him go!"

Ra'Toth's face hardened. "While I don't recognize that particular design, any Kryllin weapon capable of harming me, I am certain at this range you would kill us both. And I know you care for this traitor. Making your threat, an empty one."

Erin's eyes narrowed as her finger twitched. "You think so do you? Who is to say I wouldn't want you off my planet more?"

Ra'Toth's eyes narrowed. "Well played but I can see through your bluff. If you turn around and leave now, I may let you live. This traitor on the other hand," Ra'Toth turned his attention back to Jack and lowered the deadly tendrils closer, "will not."

Jack coughed. "Erin! Shoot! Take us both! It is the only way!"

Erin lowered the weapon. "I can't do that to you."

Ra'Toth laughed so hard his whole body shook. "Females they are the same everywhere! I do not know what you saw in her."

"Erin! Do it! Please! I am dead either way."

Ra'Toth sneered at Jack. "Give it up and accept your fate. It is a pity though, you were a good student."

"Well perhaps it is time the teacher learned something about women!" Erin shouted as she raised the weapon again and pulled the trigger.

Ra'Toth had enough time to turn his head and see the trigger being squeezed. "NO!" The energy tore from the barrel and slammed into Ra'Toth sending him careening back end over end into a tree. Jack was thrown off to the right from a combination of the blast and Ra'Toth's momentum.

Ra'Toth shrieked as his body vibrated growing larger and larger. "What did you do? I can't stop ...or ...change

…forms." He gritted his teeth with the intense pain. His normal red-black tendrils had changed to a deep green as he continued to grow. "What is happening?!" When he reached the same height as the tree his body burst into tiny spheres that evaporated.

Jack lay on the ground for a moment as a large liquid mass, then he tried to reform into his human shape. It took several tries but after a few moments he managed it. He stood up and Erin ran over to him. "Jack! Are you all right?"

"I am alive, and I shouldn't be. It should have killed us both."

"What is this thing?" Erin said holding out the energy weapon.

Jack took it and looked the device all over. "I think we had better go find out."

20

Jack and Erin entered the room, and he glared at Kan. "Kan? What is this weapon?" He placed it on one of the tables and picked up a small hand held scanner, preparing to look inside the pistol shaped object.

Kan's screen flickered as he spoke. "You told me to create a weapon to stop Ra'Toth. I did so."

"But shouldn't a normal Kryllin energy weapon have destroyed me as well? Not to mention, what it did to Ra'Toth is anything but normal."

"The weapon's design was changed based on the data I found in the backup data core from Ra'Toth's ship."

Erin's eyebrow went up. "Which is?"

"I am still analyzing it, but this much is certain: the council knows about the genetic disease deterioration and several of the oldest Kryllin have succumbed to its influence and died."

Jack gave a dismissive wave of his hand as he sat down in the chair next to the table. "That we know."

Kan's screen flashed. "Yes. However, what we did not know for certain is the council also knows the exact root cause of the genetic disease. However, while they know what the problem is, a solution has eluded them."

Erin blinked. "How can that be? If they know where in the

genome it is, shouldn't they be able to fix it? I am no geneticist but it seems like it should be simple."

Jack nodded. "You're right, it should be. It doesn't make sense."

Kan's screen flashed again. "Correct, but every attempt has resulted in accelerating the disease, and death of the patient. Considering that each death has such a huge impact for a race that can no longer procreate, the project was abandoned. At least internally. They have been looking outside of the homeworld as they assumed the solution must be there and they had time."

Jack nodded. "Yes that part they told me."

"Correct. What they didn't tell you, the disease has progressed to cause a problem with the aging of a Kryllin. Up until the last cycle it only affected the very old. But a few younger Kryllin have now appeared to age rapidly and then died."

"Hmm, while I knew the disease had progressed further causing deaths, I didn't know how it was happening."

Erin cocked her head. "Isn't that strange for a race that gets stronger as they get older? Shouldn't they be getting stronger and be able to fight it off?"

"I suspect the changes are so rapid that the body cannot cope."

Kan's screen flashed. "Correct. The council knows how it happens, the problem is they do not know why or who will be affected next."

"No wonder they are shaking in their boots," Erin said.

"If you are stating that they are afraid, you are correct."

Jack folded his hands behind his head and leaned back. "Is there anything else?"

"Not on the data core."

Jack folded his arms in front of his chest. "How does this all apply to the weapon?"

"Based on the data I found in the core, I changed the energy matrix to accelerate the genetic disease in a Kryllin."

"So he died from his body changing too fast and the bonds in his genetic structure fell apart?"

Kan's screen flashed. "Correct."

"Then how am I alive?"

"Sir, do you feel any different?"

"No, why?"

"You no longer suffer from the genetic disease."

Jack choked as he sat up. "What?"

"You gave me a sample of your bio mass earlier today to see if anything had changed. It has. The degeneration is not visible in your genome."

Jack blinked. "How is that possible?"

"I think I know how." Erin said with a sly smile.

"Oh? Do tell, this has me completely baffled. Sure with the right genetic recombination chamber, and we knew what to do, this is certainly possible. But I haven't done anything like that."

"You made love to me."

Jack squinted, looked off to the side in deep thought then turned back to find her eyes waiting. "Yes we did, but that shouldn't have done anything without–"

"And I love you."

Jack dropped the tool he was holding. It landed with a loud clang. "You … you … you do?"

She grinned. "Yes you dummy. Why did you think I wouldn't leave you?"

"Well I thought you were just trying to help your race."

"I was, but it goes much deeper than that. And I know you love me." Jack's mouth hung open, and she closed it for him. "Good you didn't deny it."

"Since the first time we made love. I knew. Only a man truly in love with his wife could care for me like you did."

"But I am not a human."

Erin stepped forward and ran her finger down his chest. "No, but you are a man."

"But it still doesn't make any sense why–"

"Jack my darling, it does if you open your eyes. Love is the key. It is something your people never considered. The love we feel, my body, and your morphing abilities combined to create the cure."

"But that is not scientific!"

"Sweetheart, let me ask you something. Can you explain love in a formula? Or scientific reason?"

"Er, no," Jack stammered.

"Well there you go. We have a saying here, love can conquer all. And I think we just proved it."

"But–"

Erin put a finger to his lips. "Shhh. Does it really matter? You are cured, we love each other and are together." Erin raised an eyebrow. "Or did you plan on leaving me?"

"Heck no! I couldn't find another woman like you if I were to live thousands of years."

Erin sighed. "I am sure you will. But I will be with you for all of my life, it won't be as long as yours I know–"

Kan's screen flashed. "It is very possible you will live to the same age."

She glared at Kan. "What do you mean? Don't tell me the changes also took away his long life?"

"Nope that is intact."

"Then what changed?"

Kan's screen flashed. "You."

"Me? But we established–"

"No you don't understand. The genetic changes didn't only affect K'lan. After I verified the changes in his genome, I assumed you were the cause, considering nothing else could account for it. I scanned your DNA when you entered the room."

Erin blinked. "You mean–"

"Correct, the Kryllin immunity to age seems to have been passed to you. I need to do more tests as there might–"

Erin jumped into Jack's lap and kissed him so passionately that he would have lost a filling, if had one. "I don't care! We have a very long life ahead of us ... together."

Jack grinned. "Yes my darling, we do. And so do the Kryllin, not to mention Earth as well."

Erin blinked as she leaned back then cocked her head. "What do you mean?"

"I can save my people as well."

"How?"

"With the before and after samples, Kan should be able to determine how to reproduce what happened to me without the need for the need for the invasive testing on humans that my people were planning. And if I transmit that to my people–"

"They can replicate the cure on your homeworld!"

Jack's grin broadened. "Exactly. And there will be no longer be a need for them to come here."

Erin squeezed Jack tighter. "Sounds like a win-win to me."

"It is, but the biggest win, is here in my arms. I love you my darling."

"And I love you," Erin said as she pulled him closer and kissed him with all that she had. Without a word, they intertwined their hands and headed for the bedroom.

A few minutes later Kan's screen flashed. "Funny they didn't ask me if I could. While I can build the communication system necessary to contact the homeworld, it would have been nice to be asked," he muttered. The fabricator lit up as antenna components started to form.

Red Warp

She looked around the room and sighed flicking her long red hair over her shoulders as she stood up. She knew that it would drain her beyond normal limits, already being so very tired, but there was little choice. They would be back soon and then her time would be up. They wanted her power, or thought her insane. While most didn't really believe, they would soon! And to think she came to *help* them! She looked around the small room again. She picked up the four heavy wooden chairs and placed them on the table that took up almost the entire space.

She sighed again and pulled the zipper of her skintight black bodysuit all the way up, past her neck. She hoped there was enough room. She had never done it in such a small space before. Looking off into the distance and with great concentration she began to run. In a circle ... faster and faster. Air began to swirl around picking up several papers that were on the table and flung them into the wind. Faster and faster she ran. "I must *DO* this!" She muttered and increased her speed again. One of the chairs flew off and were now following her swept up in the whirlwind. A storm had formed. A storm of her own making.

And with the crack of thunder a bolt shot from the center and the room reeked of ozone. She increased her speed once more but began to feel the storm's draining effect and knew she was out of time.

With a loud *KABOOOM* that shook the whole building, a warp had formed. A rip in the very fabric of space and time. She knew there were only seconds before they came running in here. The table cracked, splintered, fell in upon itself, and disappeared as the warp grew gaining strength. A microsecond later the door burst open with armed men ready to do battle, but with the storm all they could do was hang on to the door frame as the great forces pulled them horizontal.

The warp was smaller than usual, but she could not go anymore. It was enough. She ran for it and jumped into the angry swirl of color. With a loud *CRASH* it closed in upon itself and instantly the wind died. People and the chairs fell to the floor with a *thud*.

Stars in a multitude of colors streamed past her vision. She knew they were not real stars but she was beyond what her mind could comprehend, making them look like stars.

As quick as it started, it stopped. She fell to the ground on a soft patch of grass. Gazing around she saw trees, lush streams and heard birds chirping in the background. She knew it was not a matter of *where* she was but *when*. She closed her eyes and muttered "I must rest" and fell into a deep sleep.

Red awoke with a start looking up to a dark sky filled with stars and half of a moon. How much time had passed? She gazed at her self illuminating watch and silently laughed. Without looking before she closed her eyes, there was no way to know how long she had been unconscious. Could be a few hours later or more than a day.

She straightened and felt every muscle in her body

complain all at once. Looking around the area where once a vast building stood, she was reminded how risky warping was, especially since she was on the third floor. Thankfully, the warp had drifted down a little or she could have died from the fall when she arrived here ... wherever here was. No, she corrected herself, *whenever*.

Red slowly got to her feet, listening to the crickets and bullfrogs in the distance, although she thought they sounded different for some reason. She sighed thinking how she was always called Red as far back as she could remember, which wasn't very far. There was a large gap in her memory and she didn't know why. Then her head spun, the world wobbled and she realized getting up right now was not such a good idea. She fell back to the ground asleep before her head touched the grass.

Red awoke to someone shaking her violently. She blinked trying to clear her vision. Then she saw the glint of a gun shoved into her face. "*WHO* are you! And where are we?" The man waved his gun around and shouted. "Answer me! I am not in the mood for games. The building is gone, everything is gone! Where are we!"

Her vision finally cleared, and she recognized him as one of the agents that came into the room right before she jumped. He must have traveled with her. This was a first. She looked around then back at him. "I ... I ... I don't know," she stammered.

Suddenly they heard a sound. An alien sound of something very large nearby. Her blood turned to ice. She went back all right, but way too much.

The man looked around momentarily forgetting Red entirely. "What in the world was that?!"

Red quickly shushed him. "Shut up you moron or we will be a meal. Now get off of me and put that gun away. If it goes off, we are dead."

"I want to–" he said with a confused look.

"Okay let me try this again. Do you want to live?"

He looked blankly at her for a second in a state of shock. "Of course, what kind of question is that?"

"Then stop asking me stupid questions and do as I say and you might live to see tomorrow! You got that?"

He nodded slowly and got off of her and she leapt to her feet. She had been here before, and that was trying to see how far she could go. Dang them! If it wasn't for their interference in her concentration, the jump wouldn't have thrust them this far back!

The earth shook slightly as they felt a tremor. A small one, almost imperceptible, then the next one …stronger …the then the next even stronger yet.

"What is–"

Red covered his mouth. "Shut up! Do you want to get us killed?" she whispered. "Now follow me and for goodness' sake try to be quiet!" He holstered his gun, she grabbed his wrist, and they moved as quietly as they could to a thick patch of very large foliage she could just make out in the dim light. She jumped into the large ferns and pulled him in with her. Their noses wrinkled as the ferns strong scent covered them. Red just hoped it would be enough. The earth shook again more violently this time as a giant foot of a Tyrannosaurus rex landed very close to them. The beast looked around sniffing the air then leaned down to where they were hiding and sniffed again, looking confused. His head bobbed up again as he looked around. Then he put his snout down and began to push into the ferns when a loud sound froze him into place. He raised his head and gave an angry retort to the air and took off in the direction of the challenge.

"That was–"

Red slapped her hand over his mouth. "Do you ever shut up?" she whispered. "Give it another minute or two then we can move." After a few minutes, which seemed like hours in their cramped location under the ferns, she stood up. "Should be clear now. I am sure he took off after the challenger at full speed and won't be back now."

The man stood up his face glistened in the dim moonlight wet from sweat or the ferns, Red couldn't tell which. "What was that?"

"Tyrannosaurus rex. I'm sure you have heard of them."

"Of course I have heard of them! But they are long dead. So are we on some kind of movie set?"

Red snorted. "Don't I wish!"

"Well then where are we?"

Red glared at him as she sat down on a large rock nearby. "Isn't it obvious?"

The man looked blank. "No."

"Okay let me try this again, really really slowly. That was a real dinosaur. A Tyrannosaurus rex, now think for a moment. What does that mean?"

"We went back in time?"

Red raised her arms looked to the sky. "Thank you God, yes he can be taught!" She lowered her arms and jabbed a finger in the man's face. "Now if it wasn't for you, I wouldn't be in this situation."

"Because of me?" He said placing a hand on his chest. "I didn't do this to you!"

"You did! You broke my concentration! I came to try and help save your president, and what do I get? People calling me insane and think I am a terrorist. If I was a terrorist would I have been warning people? You government types have no sense at all."

"We broke your concentration?"

"Yes YOU! I should have normally spent an hour preparing for that jump, instead I had to do it blind. I only wanted to jump a little bit not this freaking far!"

"And why do you keep saying we did this? I didn't do this to you."

"You are with the FBI aren't you?"

"Well yes–"

"Well then, who are *you*?" Red felt the idiocy of the question the second after she said it.

He stiffened. "Agent James Moknkin!"

"Oh full agent, eh? And where is your access badge?" She said pointing at his chest.

James looked down to see a ripped spot on his sport jacket where his badge once hung. "Well looks like it was taken off by a whirlwind that *someone* else made!"

"And how long have you been there?"

"My first day, I–"

Red snorted and shook her head. "Just great. All the agents in the world and I get stuck with a trainee in the distant past!"

"Hey, I will have you know I graduated first in my class!"

"Well excuuuuse me. But I bet your training never covered this!"

"Er . . . um . . . no. And how did you know the ferns would shield us?"

"I have been here before. Long ago. It was a mistake. At the time I was wondering how far I could go, I shouldn't have tried it. I learned a lot about dinosaurs that the paleontologists got totally wrong. Like these ferns act like Jurassic pepper. They don't smell anything other than the ferns for awhile, but it also can make them sneeze. And believe me you don't want to be sneezed on by a dinosaur, it is really disgusting."

"I see. Now could you please tell me who you are?"

Red snorted. "I think you already know."

James rolled his eyes. "No I don't. I don't know what your case was. They called an emergency and all agents on the floor were to report to holding room 3. I happened to be a few doors down and came running."

"Lucky you." Red said as she sat down on a large rock and rubbed her sore muscles.

"Yeah lucky me," He sighed.

"Well I am Red."

"Red ...?"

"Yes Red."

"That is all?"

"Yes that is all I can remember. As far as I know I have always been called Red."

"You have amnesia?"

"Well, I'm not sure. I don't have any memories past 8 years ago. What happened before then I don't know." She shrugged and stretched cracking her back.

"I see. Now can you please get us back?"

"I'm not sure I can."

"WHAT! What do you mean you are not sure? You got us here!" James said a little more loudly than he intended.

"Well to be honest I don't know exactly how I do what I do. Only that I can and it takes a great deal of concentration and energy. And if I don't, then very odd things can happen, like this." She paused a moment to gesture to the surrounding land.

"But you said you were here before?" James said sitting down next to her on the large rock.

"Yes. I shouldn't have tried it though. I was seeing how far I could go. It was a mistake. But a bigger one than I thought. You must understand, then like now, I managed to get here in one jump. But getting back was difficult. It took over twenty jumps."

"Twenty? Twenty of those ... storms?"

"Yes. And I traveled alone. In fact I don't know how you managed to follow me. What was the last thing you remember?"

"Well ..." James looked off into the starry night that was starting to give way to morning. "As I said I heard the emergency call, and I came running into holding room 3. The door was gone, ripped right off its hinges, and I remember seeing a whirlwind. I tried to stop but couldn't. That is all until waking up here."

"Sounds like the combination of your motion and the storm carried you into the warp allowing you to follow me here. Amazing really, no one has ever followed me before." Red said as she watched the sun peek over the horizon gently waking everything around them.

"Have they ever tried?" James looked at her concerned.

"One did I think. But he never made it. Normally people are not around me when I jump. Safer for everyone."

"Well after experiencing this first hand, I have to agree."

Red jumped up from the rock and stretched again. "We

need to get going. With the sun up we are sitting ducks out here in the open. We need to find better cover."

"Can't you get us back? You said it took you twenty jumps, but you did make it. Why don't we get started now?"

Red sighed and started walking towards what looked like caves in the distance. "Look, for one thing every jump drains me. The longer the jump the more of the drain. It may take me a few days before I am up to trying again. Perhaps longer. And secondly I don't know you. The FBI was going to lock me up as a security risk and you are part of the organization. So excuse me if I don't feel like helping you."

"Why did the bureau want to lock you up? What did you do?" James said as he followed along behind her and silently wished he had worn his black sneakers instead of his dress shoes, they were not the best in this environment.

"It is what I tried to do, rather than what I did."

"Tried to do?"

"Okay here goes, I saw the president die. This allowed the vice president to take over. Unfortunately this turned out to be very bad and the decisions he made lead to a full scale nuclear war in one hundred years time. There wasn't much left of the earth after that point. I tracked the start of the whole situation to this one point in time. I thought perhaps if I traveled back and warned the FBI they could avoid it. Of course, they didn't believe me. The problem is I gave them detailed information about the president over the next few days. Where he was, who was there, exact times and dates. Something that turned out to be classified information."

"Oh I see, so they thought you were a part of the situation instead of trying to help?"

"Exactly. I told them of my ability, but of course they didn't believe me. And at that point I think that even if they did, I would have been locked up to find out how I do it. I decided I needed to get out of there and fast. I had no intention of being a lab rat." They continued walking towards a group of rocky outcroppings in the distance. By this time the terrain had already changed from a soft grassy plain to jagged rocks laying haphazardly. James stumbled and Red sighed as she helped him, yet again, to his feet.

"Can we rest? We have come a long way. Surely we are safe now?"

Red rolled her eyes. "Not yet, once we get to those caves, then we can. We are still too exposed here. You don't know dinosaurs, they rarely give up once they get your scent. Well the carnivores anyway. The herbivores you only have to worry about them stepping on you." She pulled at James' arm. "Come on will you. I thought you said you were top of your class?"

"I was. But the training didn't include early Jurassic!"

When they finally reached one of the caves, they both collapsed on its dirt floor and James immediately removed his shoes to rub his aching feet. "I don't suppose you know where the closest restaurant is?"

"Sure, thousands of years in the future," Red chuckled. "But I think I can come up with something a little closer. I noticed a tree with fruits when we came in. I will go get some of them. Will you be okay?"

James nodded. "Yes I will be fine." He said sitting down on a large rock, patting it. "All the comforts of home."

Red smiled as she turned to leave. "I will be back."

A short time later Red appeared at the cave entrance carrying two large plum colored oblong objects. Both were larger than her hands and she had to carry one under each arm. "Here you are," she said handing him one, "but be careful, some inner pods are seeds and will break your teeth. Also, if you ever find some that look like these but are shiny, don't eat those. They will kill you in one bite."

"How do you know?" He said as he chewed the sweet fruit.

"I got lucky enough to watch something else take a bite. Believe me, you don't want to try it." Red said as she broke open her fruit and popped a small yellowish oblong piece into her mouth.

"Thanks, I will keep that in mind. You said you were here before and it took twenty jumps to get back? Why so many?" James said as he finished the last of his fruit.

"Well, going forward is much more difficult than going backwards in time. I don't know why. But I do know it takes a lot more energy and concentration." Red raised her hand. "And before you ask, it still will be about another day before I can try. Believe me, I don't like being here in dinosaur world anymore than you do. But this is a lot better than Salem."

James eyes grew wide. "Salem?"

"Yes you know of the city right?"

"Of course, but how can you say this is better than Salem?"

Red laughed. "Okay, well in modern times I agree, but if you land in the middle of a witch trial looking like this from a storm what would you think just happened?"

"You are kidding? You were in Salem during the witch trials?"

"I wasn't there during the witch trials, I was the reason for them! Sadly I landed right at the feet of a judge. Of course he immediately called everyone around and shouted witch. And just my luck, he wasn't the only one that saw me land …"

Want to read more about Red and James? Then visit your favorite book store and pick up a copy of Red Warp! Available in both print and e-book editions.

Time Rock

Professor Keleeigan sat over one of his consoles tweaking several wave guides on the display. He rolled his chair over to a large piece of equipment filled to the brim with various circuits and electronics. He carefully reached inside and soldered a new chip into place. The status lights on the box continued to flash orange for a few more minutes, then blinked green. "There," he grunted, "it is finally finished." A knock at the door brought him out of his thoughts as he walked through the maze of tables and equipment that covered the lighthouse floor. Pulling open the heavy wooden door he smiled as his eyes fell upon on the young man standing in front of him. "Kim! Good you could come!"

Kim Lee stood in his usual well-worn shorts and t-shirt. "Hello Professor, your message said it was important? Why did you want to meet back here at the lighthouse so soon?"

Keleeigan grinned. "Why, to show you the fruition of our work."

Next to Kim a woman uncomfortably shifted from one high-heeled foot to another. "Fruition? How? We are a long way from testing."

Keleeigan glared at Trisia Swain. "Hardly. Or don't you

trust my work?"

Trisia shifted again in her heels. She was on her way for a fun night on the town when she received the Professor's message. She shivered as the wind blew up her blue minidress. "Professor you know that we both trust your work. It is why we agreed to join you on this project. And in secret I might add."

Keleeigan gestured for them to come inside. "Well don't just stand out there come on in. I know it is still a bit chilly after the sun sets. If we are lucky, a storm will soon follow."

Kim's eyebrow raised as he closed the door behind them. "A storm? Why would that be lucky?"

"Because my boy, a storm is what we need!"

"I don't follow you."

Keleeigan sat back down at one of the large lab tables then swiveled his chair around to face them. "Well you know we couldn't generate enough power to create a stable time-field, right?"

Trisia's eyes narrowed. "Professor is this going to take long? I had other plans for tonight."

Keleeigan laughed. "My dear it won't take long at all. If you would let me finish explaining."

Trisia's eyes lowered as they fixed on the ancient wood floor. "Sorry."

"No problem my dear. Now as I was saying, you know that the new power cell I developed wasn't quite powerful enough to open a temporal field right?"

Kim nodded. "Yes, and I thought you were going to build another?"

"Yes that was my original plan, but it will take months to build and test a new cell with these systems. You know how finicky they are."

"Yes we do, all too well." Trisia said sighing deeply. It was part of her job to try to get the systems to work together in harmony. A lot more difficult than anyone originally thought due to the intricacies of the self regenerating power cell. Having to run to the basement for each calibration on the large cell didn't make the job any easier.

"Well, I think I may have found a workaround, and it should expand the field as well."

"A workaround?" Kim said looking rather perplexed.

"Yes and it should be here soon."

"Be here soon? I still don't quite follow."

"Well we need a massive amount of power and I think I found a good source. It won't be enough for a two-way trip in this case, but it will allow testing of the theory and equipment."

Thunder boomed in the distance as the rain began to pelt against the windows. Trisia looked through the dirty glass and started moving towards the door. "Professor I am sorry but I don't have time for games, and I had plans for tonight. I need to head out before this storm gets any worse."

"But my dear this is what we need."

"You keep saying that, but we still don't know what you mean."

"You will." Keleeigan said as he punched a button opening a small door at the top of the lighthouse releasing a small weather balloon.

Kim pointed to the button. "Professor, what did you just do? I don't recognize that panel."

Keleeigan smiled. "Why I started our trip of course, don't worry this will work. I have no doubts." His words hung in the air for a microsecond before a large lighting bolt struck the weather balloon and traveled down its connecting wire to the power accumulator that Keleeigan had installed in place of the giant light. It glowed brightly as it reacted to the sudden power surge. "Okay here we go!"

Trisia's eyes widened, and she bolted for the door. "I am leaving!"

"You can't! The process has already begun!"

Trisia opened the door but just beyond it an energy field covered the exit. "What have you done?! I am getting out of here!" She yelled running to the window on the far side, her heels clicking loudly on the wood floor.

"That won't work, the field is covering the whole lighthouse."

"The whole building? But that is impossible! Our calculations indicated a small stable rip would require more than the power cell was capable of. Let alone a whole building." Kim said as he ran to the panel that showed the energy level rising and going higher than the gauge could reliably measure.

"It is possible, and I am proving it!" Keleeigan said as a light flashed and blew out under the increased load. Another panel sparked and exploded.

"Professor! You must abort this madness!" Trisia said waving her arms.

"I can't! It is too far along!" Keleeigan shouted as the building began to twist and tear as though it was made of putty. "Don't worry we are only jumping a day ahead."

"No!" Trisia shouted before she fell backwards sliding across the floor with the sudden lurch as the lighthouse surged with power flickering in and out of existence then disappearing entirely leaving only an empty hole where it once stood.

The lighthouse twisted and pulled inside the temporal field but managed to snap back into shape. Keleeigan held on to the table as all sorts of images flashed through his mind. Distant past, possible futures, but as soon as it all started it stopped. The lighthouse emerged from the temporal warp with a loud crash.

Kim sat down and shook his head. "What was that?"

"The temporal field must need an adjustment." Keleeigan said still holding on to the table. "Whew, what a ride."

"So where are we?"

"Not where, but when. Should only be one day ahead in time."

Trisia got to her feet and quickly walked to the door, eager to leave but when she got outside, nothing was as she expected it. "Um Professor, I think you had better get out here."

"What's the matter dear? Something happen to your car?"

"In a manner of speaking, it is not here."

"What do you mean? We only went ahead a day."

"I don't think so, I think we moved distance rather than time."

Keleeigan walked outside and looked at the landscape. The grass covered land stretched as far as he could see. "This is impossible, I didn't change the land coordinates, only the temporal. Yet, I don't see the coast line."

Kim sat down at one of the consoles and activated the mapping system. He tried several configurations, but they all returned the same error. "Professor I can't get a fix on any GPS satellites. It's like they don't exist."

Keleeigan walked quickly to check the screen Kim was

looking at. "Why you are right. I guess we jumped a lot farther into the future than I thought. And moved in physical location as well."

"Professor? Do you have binoculars? I think I see something in the distance," Trisia called.

"Yes, I will be right there." Keleeigan said as he grabbed his large binoculars from another table and joined Trisia outside. "Now what are you looking at?"

Trisia pointed to some spots in the distance. "Over there. I think they are moving. Cars perhaps?"

"Too slow to be cars. Not to mention too big to be seen at this distance." Keleeigan said raising the binoculars to his eyes. "Oh no! But this can't be! This is impossible, how could I have made such an error?!"

Kim ran to join them. "What do you see?"

Keleeigan passed him the binoculars. "Here take a look for yourself."

Kim focused the binoculars and gasped. "Dinosaurs!"

Keleeigan sighed. "Yes, dinosaurs."

Trisia blinked. "How? I thought you said we were going into the future?"

"I don't know my dear, I don't know. It would seem that we have gone far into the past, back before this was coastline. So we didn't move in position as I thought, only time. But a lot more than I wanted."

"Professor I hate to say this, but I think they are coming this way," Kim said still looking through the binoculars.

"Yes I suspect they will. And more will join."

"Why?"

"Because my boy, dinosaurs like temporal energy. They are attracted to it for some odd reason."

"And how do you know this?" Trisia glared at Keleeigan.

"From a friend."

"And how did this friend know?"

"Never mind, let's just say I am sure she knew what she was talking about."

"We need to get out of here." Kim said finally lowering the binoculars. "They will be here soon."

"I agree, but we need lightning for a stable temporal field. And I don't think that is likely to happen any time soon," Keleeigan said gesturing to the bright sunny day, "do you?"

"No, but we can't just sit here!" Trisia said.

Keleeigan turned to go back inside. "Nor will we. I have an idea."

"I hope it is a good one," Kim muttered under his breath.

"It is, close that door Trisia."

"Why? That won't keep them out."

"No, but a force field will."

"Force field? Are you joking?"

"Hardly, if I adjust the harmonics of the field generator that I used to produce the temporal effect it should feel like a brick wall."

"How long will it last?"

"Should give us plenty of time, enough to wait for a nice lighting bolt."

"But even if we do, how will we get back home? You still don't know why we are here in the first place."

"Oh I will find out, trust me."

Keleeigan checked several circuit boards inside the temporal guidance system as another dinosaur slammed into their makeshift shield.

"Why don't they give up?" Trisia sighed as she looked out the window. Another raptor had joined the others, making six raptors and one Tyrannosaurus rex circling outside.

"That field while protecting us, also attracts them. A double-edged sword. And I think I found the problem." Keleeigan said producing a small burnt chip from deep inside the guidance system. "It looks like this chip fried locking us on to several million years ago instead of a day into the future. Very strange considering nothing else is damaged in the system."

Trisia glared at him. "Can you fix it?"

"Sort of."

"What do you mean 'sort of'?"

"Well I don't have a lot of spare parts here. A few yes, but this is a very delicate chip with an intricate clock. I can bypass it, but I don't know what will happen then. We could end up in an even worse position."

"We may not have a choice," Kim said emerging from the basement. "I double-checked the power cell, it is down to 76% and dropping fast. I don't think we have more than a few hours before the shield gives out."

Keleeigan nodded. "Yes based on the current drain, we have about four hours left. I didn't count on the dinosaurs constantly attacking the shield. It is draining much faster than I anticipated."

"Then what do we do?"

"We try to jump as soon as I bypass this chip."

"Now? I thought you needed a lightning strike?" Kim said.

"Wait a second! You said that if you bypass that we will have no way of knowing where we are going!" Trisia said running over to grab Keleeigan's arm.

"My dear, if we don't try we will be dino dinner. Would you prefer that outcome?"

"No! Of course not!"

"Then let go of my arm so I can finish this!"

"Sorry professor." Trisia said releasing his arm looking embarrassed. "But what about the power level? You said we needed lightning?"

"Well we needed that boost to stabilize and exit, not enter the temporal field."

"Well at least we can enter … wait … if we can only enter that sounds like we will be trapped?"

"We could be. It is only a theory of mine. And I hope I am wrong."

Kim frowned. "Professor, most of your theories are proven true."

Keleeigan sighed. "I know. But what other choice do we have?"

The shield shimmered as the Tyrannosaurus bashed into it again. "Professor the power dropped to 72%, how much do we need to make the jump?"

"If it gets below 70% we won't have enough to try." He said activating a program before he stood and walked across the room. "I need to check the power accumulator upstairs. Be right back." Keleeigan said as he started to climb the winding steps. A moment later he reached the top and pulled a small pocket video recorder from his lab coat that transmitted directly to his system below.

Want to find out what happens? Then visit your favorite book store and pick up a copy of Red Warp: Time Rock! Available in both print and e-book editions.

Soulmates

Pain tiptoed though her mind as Aleshia pulled the pillow over her head to block the sunlight pouring though the window. It helped, but her head still ached. "Not again. To feel like this, I should have had too much fun last night," she muttered beneath the pillow as Miles entered. Roughly human shaped but with a large dome instead of a standard type head, Miles was one of the nicer of the Mechand models allowed for home use. He did many of the duties no one else wanted: cooking, cleaning, and making sure the refrigerator was stocked. He could be further enhanced, but Aleshia liked to do many things herself. As usual, Miles had activated his anti-grav, allowing him to float a few inches off the ground and enter quietly. "Miss Aleshia, it is time to get up." He said in his gentle, yet artificial voice.

"Ugh! Can I sleep a little more? Or at least try to?" Her words were muffled though the pillow, but not beyond Miles' recognition abilities.

"I am sorry, but you did ask me to wake you at this time. You do have that important appointment today, if you recall."

Aleshia popped up from under the pillow pushing the dull ache away for the moment. "Oh it is Tuesday isn't it? I forgot

I am meeting Mindy today. What time is it?"

"9:00am standard, your appointment is at 11:00am standard. I estimate you have enough time to ready yourself and transport there if you begin now."

Aleshia sat up and stretched. "Sometimes you take all the fun out of it, Miles."

"The fun out of what?" Miles asked still hovering by her bed.

"Never mind. I had better get ready. Mindy will be wondering if I am late. We have been looking forward to this shopping trip for quite a while."

"I do not understand why you wish to go shopping for clothing when I can create anything you might require."

"Miles, it is a girl thing. You wouldn't understand."

"A girl thing? Yes it is apparently beyond my understanding why someone would want to travel to a store halfway around the planet for items that were created using the same basic templates I have and require less expended energy to complete."

"Miles, just go make breakfast and I will be down in a few minutes."

"Yes Miss Aleshia." Miles said as he inclined his dome, then hovered out of the room.

Aleshia crawled out of bed and drug herself to the sonic shower. This morning though, the sonic didn't feel potent enough. She keyed in her code to use a ration of actual water and the jet turned on bathing her in luxurious liquid. She relished in its warm embrace for several extra minutes before turning it off and climbing out. The shower had helped push the headache back into the invisible box from where it came. She dried herself off and placed the towel in the cleaning drawer and set it to auto. Walking over to her closet, she found the dress she wanted to wear today. A strapless design with a short skirt that came to her mid thigh. Just enough to make things interesting, should she find someone to be interesting with. She then put on a pair of adjustable pumps and set the height to two inches, and the color to match the emerald dress she now wore.

Walking downstairs she found Miles had finished breakfast, and her usual place was already set. She sat down as her nose caught the wonderful scents wafting through the air. "Mmmm it smells good."

"It is your usual, synth egg, bacon, and waffles. Supplies are running low. I need to refill them in the next few days. Do you authorize me to procure more with your normal rations?"

"Yes Miles," she said while munching on the strip of bacon, "that is fine. How much will you need?"

"No more than a third of your total for the month, but I shouldn't need to acquire any more for some time."

Aleshia nodded. "That won't be a problem, I can apply for more if we need. I doubt it will be necessary though, the ration has always lasted before."

"Yes I concur, I do not believe you will exhaust the existing ration. And even then you have quite a bit on your reserve that you have accumulated from past unused totals."

"Exactly. I think ..." She dropped the fork and held her head as a sudden searing pain raced through her mind. It felt like someone was drilling into her brain with a dull razor. Almost as quickly as it began, the pain lessened and disappeared.

"Miss Aleshia? Are you all right?" Miles said as he hovered over to her.

"Yes I'm fine Miles. Thank you."

"I beg to differ. Your actions indicate another headache,

correct? That makes three this past week. May I call a med-tech this time?"

"NO! I am fine. You are not to call or notify anyone, is that clear?"

"Acknowledged," Miles said as he craned his head dome a little in Aleshia's direction, "but I really think I should call a med-tech or at least let me scan you."

"NO DOCTORS! And I do not want you scanning me either, is that clear?"

"Yes, perfectly clear."

"Good," Aleshia said as she got up from the table, "make sure you get more of that chocolate cream cake I like. We haven't had it in a long time."

"I will try, but you know that the raw materials are more resource consuming. I may not be able to with the current budget."

Aleshia waved her hand dismissively. "Just get it. I have enough back ration credits to pay for it. I can afford to treat myself once in a while."

"Acknowledged. Will there be anything else Miss Aleshia?" Miles said as he took the dirty plate, silverware, and hovered over to the sink to begin the cleaning process.

"Nope. That's all. Thanks Miles."

"You are welcome Miss Aleshia. And if I may make an inquiry, why are you wearing the impractical shoes today?"

Aleshia laughed. "Because they make my legs look good. And I am going out today."

"But you could damage yourself with such footwear." Miles said as he finished cleaning and sterilizing the dishes.

Aleshia laughed again. "You worry too much. Look these are adjustable, if I have problems I can always lower the heel. All right?"

"I suppose. However, I do not understand the reason behind them. If you are trying to attract a mate, it would be far easier to file with the central systems that you want one. I am sure with all of your attributes, you would have the desired mate within a day."

Aleshia shook her head. "All these centuries and you Mechands still do not understand us at all."

"Perhaps not. But you did build us remember?"

"Well not I, but yes our forefathers did. I never could understand why they didn't create you with better insight into us." Aleshia said as she grabbed a light coat and walked towards the door, her heels clicking loudly on the synthetic wood floor.

Miles would have shrugged if his body allowed it. "I do not know. My knowledge base is limited in that regard. Have a good day Miss Aleshia."

"Thank you Miles." She said while keying the door to lock after her.

Aleshia walked down the stairs that led from her house to the garage. Keying in her access, the force door blinked slightly, then vanished revealing her red GT3982. She always liked these kinds of doors, reliable and never needed oiling. The car recognized her when she stepped into the garage, and opened its door. She slid into the drivers seat, keyed in her access code, and the car slowly rose on its anti-grav to float out of the garage and into the bright blue sky.

She activated the Auto-Nav and dialed up the speed. Within a minute she arrived at Mindy Cotinho's house. Less than two seconds after arriving in the driveway, Mindy ran out of the combination brick and stucco building and hopped into the car. Her shiny blue dress ended just below her knees with a little ruffle encircling the hem. "Hey girlfriend, ready for some fun?"

Aleshia smiled. "Always girlfriend, always." She said as she keyed in Paris, and they took off at high speed.

"Girl you are looking really hot today. Are you trying to catch yourself one?"

While the car autopilot light blinked a perfect status check, Aleshia never totally trusted it and kept her hands on the controls. "What do you mean?" She asked, never taking her eyes off of the skyway.

"You are looking hot enough to burn through the floor, and you are asking me what do I mean? Sheesh!" Mindy said, shaking her head.

Aleshia grinned. "I just wanted to look good. You know that."

"Yeah yeah yeah, looking good is one thing. Girl you are dressed to *kill*."

"I am not!"

"You so are!"

"I am not! Hey do you want to get out and walk?" Aleshia said grinning.

"This high up I don't think so. Okay, okay, you just look good."

"Thank you."

"But personally if you wanted to get one, you should file with central systems. They would have one for you in short order I am sure."

"Well even if I *was* interested, which I am *not*, there are some things that a girl has to do for herself you know? I mean how can a machine do *that* better than us, you know?"

Mindy shook her head. "Girl you really need to get a grip.

The Mechands do everything for us, that is what they were designed for. Why not let them do it?"

Aleshia grinned. "Perhaps because I like to do a lot of things myself?"

Mindy cocked one eyebrow. "Oh? Then you *are* looking for a guy then!"

"Mindy, I am so going to get you when we land."

Mindy's grin widened. "Promises promises."

Aleshia rolled her eyes. "I still will."

"Uh-huh." Mindy said as they approached Paris. "Oh I always love looking at this city from up here."

"So do I. Where shall we go first?"

"Oh I don't know. How about Calgone's Dresses and More, first and then hit Nicolette's Lingerie?"

Aleshia raised an eyebrow. "Lingerie? Now look who's trying to do it 'herself'."

"I am not! Her bras just fit me better. They look great too I admit."

"Uh-huh. Why don't you just have your Mechand make you one that fits, they should be all the same raw materials after all?"

"Because he can't seem to get it right. I know they should be all the same, but I just like hers better okay? And since when did this conversation go from you being hot to me?"

"When you started talking about hot underwear," Aleshia chuckled.

"I did not say anything about 'hot underwear'," Mindy said giggling.

"Sure, sure you didn't." Aleshia said as she began the landing sequence. A few minutes later they found themselves in one of the better clothing sellers in Paris. The floors were solid synth marble that must have taken some time to produce. Several nearby stores had gilding over the archways. Each window held a high definition, articulated hologram and indistinguishable from the real thing. The holograms switched between various models in several different dresses. Mechands could do many things, but one never looked good in a dress. Their stiff movements always gave it away.

They walked in through an arch that said 'Calgone's Fine Dresses' in rich lettering. One of the latest Mechands hovered up to them. She looked almost human, and could even pass for one, except for the ability to hover several inches off of the ground. "Good day, welcome to Calgone's, how may I be of assistance?" She said with a thick French accent.

"Yes, do you have any specials today?" Aleshia said while still glancing around the large store.

The Mechand nodded. "Yes we do. One of the original designs is being deprecated and removed from our offerings. It is available today at a 30% discount."

"May we see it please?"

"Of course, follow me." The Mechand gestured then hovered off in another direction. Aleshia followed with Mindy right behind her. "It is this one." The Mechand said pointing to a dress currently occupied by an actual mannequin.

Aleshia looked at the dress, shiny black matte with a deep plunging neck and a high hemline. It was designed to show off a woman's curves perfectly. "Very nice. May I try it on?"

The Mechand backed up a bit. "I can already tell that it will fit you perfectly. There is no need to actually wear the dress."

"Yes there is. She wants to see what she looks like *in* it," Mindy said.

Aleshia nodded. "Yes. May I try it on?"

"Very well." The Mechand said as it hovered up and carefully removed the dress from the display and placed it in Aleshia's hand. "You can change behind the curtain." She said pointing to a curtain pulled across a small recessed area in the wall.

"Thank you." Aleshia said as she walked over behind the curtain, unzipped her current dress, stepped out of it, slipped carefully into the new one, and walked out. "Well what do you think?"

Mindy made a gesture as though her finger was burning. "Hot girl, very hot. But why didn't you zip it up?"

"I couldn't find how to close the zip. Tried pulling it but it wouldn't budge."

The Mechand hovered over and pointed. "That is a special dress. If you place your thumb on the lower hem at the bottom right, it will activate the zipper."

Aleshia placed her thumb on the bottom edge near the right side of her leg and she heard a tiny beep. A second later she felt the zipper raise up as though a pair of invisible hands were pulling it. "Very nice, I don't need help to get in or out of this."

"Yes, it also has some of our latest features, including stockings."

Aleshia blinked. "Stockings feature?"

"Yes, place your thumb on the left side at the hemline, that will active the heads up display."

Aleshia pressed the hidden button, and an image flashed into her eye displaying various features. With her eye movement she activated the stockings, and she felt something slither up her legs covering them. Looking down she saw a pair of black sparkly stockings that matched the dress perfectly. "Wow I like this." She said finding an option to raise the hemline a bit more. Still another option added a nice pattern to the calf section of the stockings. "This must be one of the latest designs, why is it on sale?"

"It has remained unsold for two hundred consecutive days. Our store policy puts everything on sale after that point." The Mechand responded in its usual flat tone.

"How much?" But when the Mechand quoted the price her heart fell. "That is more than three months ration credits. I can't afford that." She said shaking her head.

Mindy stood back looking Aleshia up and down. "But it does look so good on you."

"I know, but that is just too much." Aleshia said as she pressed the hidden control to start the zipper lowering.

"Wait, didn't you tell me you had some in reserve?"

"Yes but that would take all of it, I am not going to spend it all on one dress! I might need it later."

"Look girlfriend, I have some reserve too. How about I pay for half?"

"I can't let you do that. It's too much!"

"Please? You have helped me enough in the past and I never did pay you back."

"And I didn't do it for payback, just to help a friend."

"Yes and I want to help a friend now. So you will you let me?"

"All right, all right, you win." Aleshia said as she slipped behind the curtain and carefully slipped out of the black dress and into her previous one, then stepped out.

"Hey why don't you wear it out?"

"Perhaps because it is so expensive?"

"Well if you are never going to wear it because it is so expensive, maybe we shouldn't get it," Mindy said grinning.

Aleshia laughed. "All right you win, I will wear it out." She said as she disappeared behind the curtain again, only to emerge a moment later wearing the black dress. She then keyed her green heels to color shift to black.

Mindy whistled. "Oh hush you." Aleshia said as the Mechand hovered over.

"Please prepare for palm scan to pay for the item." The Mechand said and they both raised their palms. A high intensity red light extended from its forehead, flashed over both of their hands, and vanished. "Accounts verified, the amount has been deducted. Thank you for shopping at Calgone's." The Mechand said before she carefully placed Aleshia's old dress in a Calgone's bag. The bell rang as another set of customers entered the store and she floated over to greet them.

Aleshia grabbed the bag, and they headed out of the store. As they walked passed the new customers the tall blonde woman spoke. "Oh that girl has a lovely dress, I wonder how much it is?"

Aleshia turned to face her. "It was a lot, but I am sorry, I got the last one."

The woman blinked. "Excuse me?"

"Didn't you just ask how much this dress was?"

"No, I don't think so, though I was wondering. I must have said it without realizing. My apologies."

Aleshia waved her hand. "No need. I have done that before too. Have a good day."

Outside Mindy pulled her closer. "Girl, she didn't ask that."

Aleshia blinked. "She must have. I heard her clearly, as if she spoke in my ear."

Mindy shook her head. "No, she didn't. I didn't hear

anything, and her lips didn't move. Are you sure you are feeling okay?"

"Yes, I had a headache this morning, but I am fine now. I must have imagined her saying it. Probably because I am self conscious wearing this thing. It is so expensive."

"Will you stop already! You wanted it, I saw that look in your eye. You have it and look great in it. Just enjoy okay?"

Aleshia grinned. "Okay okay girlfriend, I will. I just–" Aleshia pitched forward grabbing her head as a sudden stab of pain overtook her.

Mindy lurched forward to grab her. "Are you okay?"

Aleshia shook her head as if to clear it. "Yes, I just had a sudden headache, then dizziness. It's gone now though."

"We need to get you checked out."

"No! I am fine. Probably something I ate."

Mindy cocked an eyebrow. "I don't know, you said you had one earlier, and now another."

"Look I am fine okay? I am not going to let a little headache that only lasted a second ruin our trip. We have been wanting to come here for months."

"All right," Mindy said as she hugged Aleshia then looked into her eyes, "but anything more and we go home. Deal?"

"Deal, and thank you."

"Hey what are girlfriends for?" Mindy said with a smile as wonderful smells wafted through the air. "Mmm that smells wonderful. What do you say we go get some of that? My treat?"

Aleshia sniffed the air. "Oh my fresh lasagna, bread and," she sniffed the air again, "chocolate! Deal. You know I can't resist chocolate."

They walked down the road, their heels clicking loudly on the sidewalk. Being a warm spring day, they were both enjoying the short walk to the restaurant on the corner. Upon entering they found a wonderful quaint place that looked like one out of the history vids. The tile floor was buffed and shone brightly. The dark maroon walls were lit by lamps every few feet. The tables were all covered in fine linen, with elegant place settings upon them.

"Let's get out of here," Aleshia whispered, "this is too expensive."

"Hey, I said it was my treat, and I meant it. How often *do* we come to Paris? Hmm?"

Aleshia looked into her eyes and what she saw there washed away her objections. "Okay, but next one is mine. Deal?"

Mindy smiled. "Deal. Now let's find a table."

A moment later they were seated at one of the corner tables as another very human looking Mechand dressed in an old-fashioned tuxedo, slowly walked over to them. "Hello and welcome to Chez Allard. What would you like?"

"Do you have a special today?" Aleshia asked.

"Yes we do. Salmon lasagna with a side of garlic bread, and chocolate strawberry fondue for dessert."

"That sounds wonderful. I will take that, how about you Min?"

Mindy glanced at the French menu and decided against asking for more options. The special did sound good. "Okay make that two of the special please."

The Mechand waiter bowed. "Yes of course. Excusez-moi, I will be back in a moment."

I have finally found you. After years of searching, I have finally found you.

Aleshia blinked. "Excuse me?"

Mindy looked up from the menu and its eye catching design swirls. "Huh? What?"

"You just said you finally found me."

"No I didn't."

"Yes you did. I heard you as plain as day."

"No, I didn't. Are you sure you are feeling okay? I think we should go home."

"I am fine, and I could have sworn you said ... never mind."

You did hear me. I have been looking for you for a long time. I am not speaking vocally. We are speaking through our minds.

"What?" Aleshia said looking around.

"What what?" Mindy said giving her a strange look.

I am here. I will always be here. But if you wish to see me, look in the corner on the far right.

Aleshia turned toward her right and in a corner booth on the opposite side of the room, a man sat gazing intently at her. He was dressed very simply with black pants, white shirt and a black jacket. He smiled as their eyes met and it sent a shiver through her.

Yes it is I. You see me now.

"Who are you?"

"Who is who?" Mindy asked.

"That man over there in the corner." Aleshia gestured with her head to avoid attracting attention.

"Are you talking to him? Girl since when do you talk to strange men that never said anything to you in the first place. Never mind trying to talk to them from across the room!"

"But he did talk to me. I just–"

Mindy had enough. She got to her feet and pulled Aleshia to hers. "Okay that is it, we *are* going home. I don't know what is going on, but we *are* going home."

Aleshia rubbed her temples as they started walking towards the door. "I don't know. I–"

Don't leave. Please, not yet!

"That is enough. I am going home. Leave me alone." Aleshia said as they left the restaurant, Mindy pulling her all the way.

I will find you. No matter where you go, I will find you.

Outside Aleshia quickened her pace. "Okay let's get back to the car." She said as they walked along the sidewalk.

Mindy leaned closer. "I don't mean to alarm you, but that guy is following us."

"Get ready to run."

"I can't. Not in these heels, and neither can you."

"I can lower mine, don't worry."

Mindy rolled her eyes. "Oh figures I would forget to wear my adjustables. But then again I didn't expect to be running from men today. Running to me maybe, but not the other way around."

"Don't worry, I think he is only interested in me. You keep going and I will meet you back at the car after I lose him."

"Are you nuts?"

"No, and I don't want him knowing where our car is, or pulling my name from the ID tag. Okay?"

Mindy nodded. "Okay that makes sense. But how do I get in? Didn't you lock it?"

"The handle will open to you, don't worry."

"But!"

Aleshia gave her a squeeze. "Don't worry girlfriend I will see you in a few minutes." She shoved the bag into Mindy's hand and darted off down a side street. With his target out of sight the pursuer lost all interest in Mindy and ran after Aleshia who had already lowered her heels, making fast progress down the street.

She took a quick look back and ducked into another restaurant. A Mechand by the door started into his usual greeting. "Welcome to–"

"Never mind that. Do you have a back door?"

The metal faced machine nodded. "Yes, it is that way," he said pointing.

"Thank you." Aleshia darted for it breathing hard. A moment later she found herself in a back alley. Mentally she thought of which direction the car was and headed east. She didn't dare turn back and see if he was still there or not. She exited on another street, turned again into another dress shop and did the same as before by going out their back door. After doing this three more times, she had difficulty remembering which way to go. Eventually she remembered to check the suns position and went east. After going down a few streets, she got her bearings and found the car right where she left it. Mindy was already inside, waiting.

Aleshia hopped into the drivers seat and keyed in the ignition before Mindy could say a word.

"Is he still there?"

"I don't know and I don't want to know." Aleshia said gasping for air as the car lifted into the sky and she engaged the overdrive. The sudden acceleration shoved them back into their seats and she keyed in Mindy's house into the navigation system.

"Do you have any idea who he was?" Mindy asked.

"No, and I don't want to know."

"Are you sure? You seemed to look like you wanted to back in the restaurant."

"Yes I am sure. Believe me I am sure. We will be home soon, I took the express route. And I am sorry I ruined our trip."

Mindy grabbed Aleshia's knee. "Girl you didn't ruin our trip. That guy did. And we will go to Paris again right?" she said smiling.

"Yes we will."

"Right, so don't worry about it. Just enjoy that great dress you are wearing."

Aleshia looked down and smiled. "You know I almost forgot. Thank you again girlfriend. I love it."

"You are welcome. But you have to make me a promise."

"Which is?"

"You show me the guy you get with that dress. Deal? And I want *all* the details. Got it?"

Aleshia laughed. "You got it girlfriend."

A short while later they landed at Mindy's house. "You going to be okay?" She asked, her face full of concern.

"Sure. I am going home, have Miles draw me a hot bath, and forget all about him."

"Okay. See you tomorrow?"

"You bet." Aleshia said as she flew off to her house a few blocks down the street.

Want to find out who this strange man is? Is Aleshia going crazy? Then pick up a copy of Soulmates! Available in both print and e-book editions.

About the Author

Don is the author of six science fiction novels and many more short stories. He lives in the USA where he continues to dream up more fantastic worlds for you to enjoy. When not writing, he can usually be found devouring another science fiction book, TV series, or movie.

Other works by Don DeBon:

Red Warp

In a race against time the casualty could be your life.

If you could travel through time with just yourself and no machine needed, would you?

Meet Red, a woman with a amazing gift, the gift of passing though time and space without the need of any bulky equipment. The places she has seen, the people she has helped will blow your mind.

Now meet James, just your average newly minted FBI agent minding his own business until he is thrust headlong into Red's world. A world he didn't ask for, but one that hit him in the face full force. Can they get along long enough to survive?

Time Rock

Time Travel. Blessing or curse? One man thinks he has it all figured out but what began as a simple test has turned into a nightmare. With his equipment failing all around him, only Red and James can save him. Can they reach him in time?

Soulmates

Mechands . . . everyone has one. The metal race built by man to serve our every need. But Aleshia is about to find out they are not the benevolent protectors that she has always been taught. And who is this strange man in her dreams? The man who actually exists and reveals the whole world is not as she thought.

Word of mouth is crucial for authors. If you enjoyed this book, would you consider leaving a review? It is very much appreciated.

Amazon USA
http://www.amazon.com/

Amazon UK
http://www.amazon.co.uk/

Goodreads
http://www.goodreads.com

Connect with the Author
Email: writer.don.debon@gmail.com
Website: http://www.dondebon.com
Twitter: @DonDeBon
Google+: +DonDeBon

This Edition Published 2016 by
DBDigital Publishing

ISBN 978-0-9881783-9-7
ISBN 978-0-9881783-8-0 (ebook)